THE SEVEN
BOOK ONE OF THE

Robert Ryan

Copyright © 2020 Robert J. Ryan
All Rights Reserved. The right of Robert J. Ryan to be
identified as the author of this work has been asserted.
All of the characters in this book are fictitious and any
resemblance to actual persons, living or dead, is coincidental.

Cover design by www.damonza.com

ISBN: 9798655271869
(print edition)

Trotting Fox Press

Contents

Prologue	3
1. Smoke in the Air	12
2. The King's Men	24
3. Into Darkness	29
4. Time for Answers	37
5. The Kingshield Knights	43
6. Like a Warrior	49
7. Marked for Death	56
8. I'll Kill You, Boy	62
9. I Hate Them	66
10. White Fire	75
11. Colder than Ice	83
12. You Are Your Own Man	89
13. The Illusion of Reality	105
14. The Best Sort of Illusion	110
15. I Serve No Kingshield Knight	115
16. Older Than Faladir	122
17. A Place of Power	130
18. A Dead Man	140
19. We Fear Nothing	144
20. Shadow Hunter	152
21. With My Life	158
22. Ill Tidings	168
23. The Hypocrisy of Politics	171
24. Advice is in Vain	175
25. A Ring of Standing Stones	182
Appendix: Encyclopedic Glossary	193

Prologue

Halls of Lore: Chamber 2. Aisle 31. Item 369
General subject: Founding of the city of Faladir
Topic: Establishment of the Kingshield Knights
Author: Ancient legend translated by Careth Tar

War straddled Alithoras like a vulture hulking over a carcass. To the south, swords flashed and blood watered the trodden earth instead of rain. To the north, armies marched, the pounding of their boots the drum of death, their banners clouding the sky with the shadow of evil. In the west, the races of humanity were smitten as metal is beaten between hammer and anvil. There, in their homeland, they possessed only ruined dreams, gnawing hunger and soul-eating poverty.

The east alone offered hope, and thither they fled. But hope burned to ash, and was blown back in their faces as a choking wind.

They found only more war, and despair clawed at their hearts. Yet humanity was a hardy race, used to brutal treatment and the ill chances of the world. They took up their swords again. Their anguish they crushed beneath wills of iron. And still they kept hope alive like a spark against the night, for a foretelling was made, a prophecy born in the darkness of ruin, that at the end of their long travails a bright future would dawn.

Hope that should have died lived on, and it gave them reason to endure. And the frail spark they nurtured flared when they met the immortal Halathrin, they who in our time are named elves.

Bright were the eyes of the elves, and their faces were fair, and the wisdom of their thought reached deeper than humanity's. Immortal and lordly as they were, wealthy in the ownership of jewels and metals that came of the earth and the crafting from them of beautiful things, still they took pity on the downtrodden newcomers and marveled at their courage.

The elves shielded humanity from the worst of the wars, allowing them to recover and grow strong again. Then humanity girded their swords, and they hefted their spears once more, and they marched to war beside the elves as allies. In time, they became the fiercest warriors in the elven armies, for they spent their blood and lives freely in service to those who had helped them. They became known as the Sword of the Halathrin, and it was a title of honor.

The *Elù-haraken*, the Shadowed Wars, those battles are named, and more is forgotten of them than is remembered. And this is well, for they were a time of darkness unsurpassed, where evil held sway over much of the land. No bird nor beast, no race of humanity nor get of monster, no elf nor dwarf nor sorcerer nor wizard, no dragon that flew the midnight skies nor crawled in the deeps of the earth was not divided to one side or the other, not locked in a death-battle against enemies.

Elùdrath, the Shadowed Lord as he was called, drew creatures of evil unto him, and he gave them power that they may smite their enemies, and he put lies on their lips, poison in their bites, fire in their breath and steel in their hands that they may conquer and rule the world under his dominion.

But against the evils of the world, Halath, Lord of the Elves, set himself. A great king he was, and his nation followed him to war. Against the dark they made light. Against despair they kindled hope. And they drew others to them who would not bow to the shadow and would rather die than suffer evil to prosper.

One race of humanity, the Camar, grew close to the counsels of the great king, and that people grew wise, and they learned lore that opened their minds to the mysteries of the world. This lore, they knew, would serve them well in the days to come.

It came to pass that the Shadowed Lord was defeated, his armies laid low, his stratagems countered, his traps sprung and his followers scattered across the land. He was killed, and yet also was Halath slain.

The land knew hope, but those who lived mourned the passing of an age. They grieved for loved ones buried in hurried graves. And they sorrowed at the passing of so many fair things that did not survive the storm and whose like will never be seen again.

The Shadowed Lord was said to be dead. Others claimed that though dead, the evil he spawned lived on and would harry the races of Alithoras for long whiles yet to come. Some few foretold that Elùdrath would rise once more in the future, though none knew when, or how.

Few cared. The troubles of their days were a greater burden than the possible troubles of the future. Only elves and lòhrens, wise men who possessed use of wizardry, set guards and wards against Elùdrath's return. And they watched and waited. And they watch and wait still.

The Camar moved further east, and they prospered, and the knowledge the elves had passed to them flourished in days of peace. This was nurtured by the lòhrens who offered sage counsels and protection against the sorcerers who still lived.

Ever east the Camar roamed, and many reached the gray sea that crashed into the farthest shores of Alithoras.

And there, those hardy people who once dwelt in rude huts or laid themselves down to sleep beneath the glittering stars, built themselves fair cities, and they established wide realms, and they raised proud kings to rule them. And there also they made bulwarks against the scattered evils of the land that yet attacked them at times.

Esgallien was one such city, and even the elves marveled at what the Camar had wrought and the uses to which their gifts of knowledge had been put. But it is not said that the elves visited further east. Few, or none, ever saw white-walled Camarelon, nor many-spired Faladir, nor Red Cardoroth far to the north, yet still nigh the sea.

Many-spired Faladir shone as a gem, and its walls gleamed and the points of its spires glittered like starlight shot from a bow into the heavens. But it was one such place where the scattered evils of the world gathered, and though bereft of their master, they grew in power and came in force from surrounding hills, forests and dark places of the earth to assail the city. And sorcerers were among them, and they possessed a *Morleth* Stone.

Of old, the Shadowed Lord crafted some few of these. And they were talismans of great evil. Black they were, of diverse sizes and strengths, and their puissance was gained from the lives of sorcerers who sacrificed themselves to make them. Their sorcery and life became one with the stone.

In the Elù-haraken most were destroyed, but against Faladir the sorcerers raised one. And this was smaller than many, being able to fit into the hand of a child, but its power was the greatest.

Faladir came near to falling, and a mighty battle ensued that ran a day and a night and until noon the next. But at the end King Conduil, his retinue about him and his eyes blazing, led a charge against the enemy. With him came a lòhren, shielding him from magic, and the king reached the chief sorcerer, whose fist was held high with the Morleth Stone within to work some spell, and he hewed off the dark one's hand and slew him, and his sword hissed with steaming blood. And the enemy dispersed, fleeing into the dark places of the world, but the Camar were spent, their army dwindled, and they harried them not.

But Conduil seized the Morleth Stone from the dead hand of the sorcerer whose twisted fingers still writhed about it, and he felt the touch of its evil, and he cast it down again.

"This thing I shall destroy," he swore.

But the lòhren slowly shook his head. "I fear not, sire. That is not its fate, though we wish it. This thing, and the evil it holds, will endure so long as Faladir stands."

Conduil was not persuaded. But his oath he could not keep, for thrice he struck the stone with his sword, and no matter that it lay on rock no harm came to it. But on the third stroke, his elven-wrought blade shattered, and yet the black stone remained unharmed.

Thereafter, the king ordered all manner of attempts be made to break it. To forges it was taken for the heat of fire to melt it. It was cast from the top of a tower unto the stone below. Smiths caught it in vices and beat it with mighty hammers, and they bathed it long whiles in acid. But no attempt broke it, nor even marred its dark surface.

Conduil grew angry. And he went again to the lòhren. "Can you not destroy this thing with your power? Being made by sorcery, surely then wizardry must be able to unmake it?"

"It is not so," Aranloth answered. But seeing the anguish of the king, he bade him stand back. Then he worked his magic, and he summoned white flames hotter than any furnace, and the Morleth Stone was hemmed all around by his power. And when he was done, the stone of the floor had melted and run like mud on a slope, yet still the talisman of evil sat unharmed.

"It is as I foretold," Aranloth declared. "This stone will endure as long as Faladir stands."

"Then must my people also endure its foul sorcery that long? Shall I not rather cast it into the sea or into some bottomless crack of the earth instead?"

Then Aranloth counseled him. "Whatever is cast aside may be picked up again, and whatever is lost may be found. And there is a power in this stone that calls to creatures of the shadow. Ever they will seek it out."

The king's anger subsided. "What must be done then?"

"This only, for no other choice remains. Keep the stone, but guard it well. Evil will search it out. The covetous will try to claim it. The ambitious will lust for its power. Like moths to a flame they will come, but it will be your task, and the task of your line to protect it, to keep it out of the hands of those who would use it for harm. It will shape you, and the realm, now and hereafter."

The king looked at the stone, and there was wariness in his glance, for he understood this would be no easy duty to perform, but there was determination also.

"And in this way shall I keep my people safe?"

"It will be so. Unless you fail in your duty."

"I shall not fail."

"No, you will not. Yet the task will be difficult, and the passing of the years will make it more so. It will be a burden without end, and it will weigh you down, and those who come after."

"Even so, I shall do this thing. I swear it."

And then Aranloth drew deep of his wisdom, and of his compassion also.

"It is a great task, but you need not carry it out alone. This is what I advise."

And the wizard counseled him then, and the king heeded him.

"An order of knights I will establish. And they will be the greatest warriors in the realm. And they will occupy a tower, and there at least one at all times will guard the stone. Their number will be six, and I shall call them the Kingshield Knights, for they will fulfill my will and guard that which must be guarded."

Aranloth thought deeply. "It is not enough that they be great warriors," he said at length.

"What else must they be?"

"The lure of the stone is strong. It will tempt the knights. Therefore, they must be not only great warriors, but men of honor and kindness. Let them learn also poetry and philosophy and all the arts according to their natural talents. This will strengthen their minds so they become as sharp and true as their blades."

The king saw the wisdom of this. But he knew there would be more. The task of the knights demanded it.

"And finally," Aranloth said, "that which they protect is a thing of magic, and some of those who seek it will possess sorcery. If the knights are to fulfil their duty, let them also learn of the mysteries."

"You would make them wizards also?"

"No. One person cannot be all things. Yet still these knights will have training. They will know how to defend themselves against magic, and to accomplish that which ordinary men cannot. And I will be their teacher."

This troubled the king, for he distrusted magic. Yet also he was glad, for his burden was lightened. And he took up the stone and went away to begin the task of his life and of his line to follow after. And he was the first knight, and he chose five others after long searching.

But the lòhren was wise, and he knew the hearts of men. And when the king had gone, he prophesized again, and there was none to hear him save a manservant in the palace who later told his tale.

"Strong as you are," Aranloth muttered, his gaze lingering where the king had stood, "you will perish even as all mortal flesh. But the evil in the stone will never subside, and it will endure, and through the long years it will ever tempt its guardians. And a day will come where that order of knights who represent the best of men will succumb, and evil will enter into the realm."

"What will happen then?" the manservant asked.

Aranloth turned to him, as though unaware that he had been there. "Then evil will rise again, and the kingdom, and all the lands beyond it, will stand in peril."

"Is there no hope then? Will evil always return?"

The lòhren closed his eyes, as if in trance. "How can it not? For darkness is in the heart of humanity as well as light, and both shape all that we touch. But against the failing of the six knights, I say now a *seventh* will arise at the time that fate calls. And that knight will be the greatest of them all. In that knight, the hope of the land will reside."

Aranloth strode away then, and soon after the king raised a high tower and there established his knights. And the land knew peace and prosperity, if even at whiles strange lights were seen atop the tower.

The knights made it a habit to ride the land, they and those who succeeded them, though never all at once, and they were the best of men. They brought wisdom with them, and helped heal the sick and settle disputes. Honor and praise followed as their shadow.

But the evil of the stone did not sleep, and the lòhren's prophecy was but dimly remembered, and the stars wheeled in the sky as the years passed, and the king died. And soon both king and prophesy became legend.

The long years marched ahead after that, century after century, and legend turned to myth.

But the knights lived on.

1. Smoke in the Air

Faran listened to the forest as he walked down the lonely trail. It was quiet, and he matched its breathless silence with his own.

Dusk was the best time of day. It was a time of change though, and he felt that now, more than ever. The sun had just dipped below sight. The long shadows of the tall trees, beeches mostly, but there were clusters of rowan and ash as well, fell over his path like the shadows of giants.

The village he had come from lay miles behind him in a different valley. His own village lay miles ahead, in a valley of its own.

He was in the wild here, upon a ridge between the two valleys, and as much as he loved his life as a hunter, and the solitude of his craft, he looked forward to a hot meal and the comfort of the bed in his little cottage.

It was not hunting though that had sent him toward Durnlik Village this morning before the sun rose. It was his skill with his hunter's bow. No one was a better shot in a dozen villages all around, and he had proved that by winning the archery tournament at the district fair the last three years running. This was valuable, because it meant that when he was not hunting, he could earn coin teaching his skill at both making bows and shooting them in many settlements all around.

He resisted the urge to string it now. He did hold it tightly, though. He loved wild and lonely places such as this, but he felt the trees watching him. Or rather, something within the concealment they offered.

Foolishness. It was not even dark yet. At least not properly. He was just tired and looking forward to home too much.

But the memory of several conversations drifted through his mind. The innkeeper in Durnlik had mentioned it. Some of the youths that he had taught today how to select bow staves from yew trees had been talking of it. And the farmer whose land they wandered seeking those staves had downright warned him. *There be strangers about, lad. Asking questions and offering coin for answers. Not just coin. Gold coin. That isn't natural. And a mean look they have too. Like a fox eyeing off ducks in a tree. Stay clear of them, that's what I say. Them and their gold both.*

Faran had never yet met a farmer who spoke well of strangers. But he had not met one either whose judgment was not shrewd.

It was a worry, but he shrugged it off. The woods were his home, as much as or even more so than the little cottage he had inherited from his parents in the village. Still, his thoughts turned to what he had heard days ago from the village drunkard. *A bat I saw, gliding silently over the village green. A bat, big as a man, and fear enough filled the sky to sober ten drunk men. I swear it.*

The old drunkard was a kindly man, in his way, but he was not to be believed. Yet still, there was fear in his eyes when he spoke, and rumor was he drank at home now and not the little village inn.

More foolishness. And nothing to connect them, but Faran quickened his pace. It would be well into the night before he reached his cottage, but the sooner the better.

He was at the high point of the path now. The valley of his village came into sight, though late afternoon shadows blanketed it even more so than up where he walked on the ridge.

Dromdruin the valley was called, and his village with it. The taller ridge stretched away to his right, the highest six hills that stood out from it, their rocky tops free of trees, were called the Six Knights. The left ridge was shorter and more rounded, and covered in trees, though there were more oaks there than beeches.

Through the middle of the valley ran a stream, fed by springs in the rocky slopes. But the soil to either side of the stream was good, and he saw the patchwork of many farms there. Some fields were ploughed, others sown to oats and wheat, while the remainder pastured the white cattle of the district.

There were a few roads too, but these were more paths than proper roads. The people of the district did not travel much, and few were the tinkers and merchants that came to them. They were a good way from the city of Faladir. Nor did the village want much contact with the outside world. The residents prospered just as they were, though they did like to hear the news of what was going on in the city. Mostly bad lately.

Faran looked to the center of the valley. A vast wood lay there, and the village of Dromdruin was set within it. The stream ran close though, the fields to either side the pride of the valley, for that was the most fertile land of all. But they were narrow strips to each side of the water, and the trees grew up thick nearby.

He could not see the village. It was hidden away in the wood, just the way those who lived there liked it. But he marked the spot where it lay, and then paused.

A plume of smoke was beginning to rise. It had not been there earlier, but it was growing quickly.

Perhaps some villager had lit a bonfire. Fires were rare in the village though, except for inside cottage hearths. There was too much risk of the forest catching alight.

Sometimes when the smithy was busy the smoke gathered above it thickly. That could be it.

Faran moved ahead. But he was uneasy, and the long strides of his walk turned into a loping run that he could keep up for miles.

The dark grew about him. He was not sure when the long shadows of the trees turned into night, but when he glanced up, he saw that the thin strip of clear sky above showed a scattering of stars.

He ran ahead, glad that the way was all downhill from here, and even after the long day feeling a flow of strength in his body. He was lean and strong, and he had to fight down the urge to run at speed. That was a temptation, but it was better to go slow all the way than to wind himself halfway and walk the remainder. Not to mention the risk of tripping and falling in the dark.

It was full night now, but his eyes had adjusted. Even so, he only just saw the shadow ahead detach itself from the trees and step silently onto the path ahead of him.

He drew to a stop, wishing his bow was strung. But it would serve as a staff at need, and without thought he slipped a knife into his left hand as well.

The shadow stepped toward him. He gripped the hilt of the knife tighter and held it higher, the cold steel of its blade pale in the starlight.

"Choose one, Faran. Knife or bow. But you can't use both at the same time."

He felt like an idiot. He was a hunter, not a warrior, but even so he should have known better. Nerves. That's what he put it down to. But there was no reason to be uneasy. He knew that voice.

"Is that you, Ferla?"

She stepped forward. A hunter like him. Orphaned like him, but a few years older, and always willing to treat him like a younger brother.

The pale skin of her face gleamed now, and he glimpsed a hint of her red hair beneath her hood.

"Put the knife away, Faran. Or I'll take it from you and shave you with it. That's if you can even grow a beard yet."

He had been shaving for some years now, and she knew it. He was an adult, but she sometimes treated him as a child. But he *was* a little in awe of her, and she just might do what she said. She had all the skill at fighting that he lacked. So he slipped the knife into its sheath quickly.

"What are you doing here?"

"Hunting," she answered. "But without luck. Then I saw smoke in the valley, and heard someone running behind me. I'm glad it was you."

"I saw the smoke too. Do you think something is wrong?"

"I don't know. I was on my way back when I heard you coming."

"Why did you hide? You scared me coming out of the trees like that."

She shrugged, but up close now he saw the tightness around her eyes. She might have heard the same rumors he had. No wonder she had hidden, but no good would come from pressing her on that.

She did not answer anyway. "Only one way to find out," she said.

Turning, she started to move back down the path, and he saw the glint of a knife in her hand as she sheathed it in her belt. She *had* been scared. And she had rebuked him for drawing his knife even though she had done the same herself. But that was another topic best left alone.

Together, they loped down the track, shoulder to shoulder and running with the smooth gait of hunters accustomed to traveling long distances to find quarry. They seldom hunted in their home valley. That way, if sickness or injury ever struck them down, there would be game left close to home.

They did not speak as they ran, and for the first time he noticed that Ferla's bow was strung. He wondered if she had been stalking quarry before she saw the smoke, or if this was yet another sign of her unease.

It could be either, but he felt calmer himself for having someone with him, and he knew they were probably worrying about nothing. After all, nothing much of note ever happened in the village, and if a fire had broken out by some accident, there were plenty of people to see it and put it out before it had much chance to spread into the trees.

They ran on, and the night grew deep about them. There was nothing to hear save the scud of their boots on the earthen track, and nothing to see but the dim way ahead of them and the still shadows of the stately beeches all around.

They left the slopes behind, and reached the flat ground of the valley bottom. Here, they slowed, for the trees grew taller and thicker, and the shadows deeper. It was hard to even see the dirt track, still less any fallen branches or rocks that might trip them.

But Ferla did not just slow. After a little while she stopped altogether, and she reached out with a hand on his shoulder to make sure he stopped as well.

He was not sure why. But then he heard what she must have heard even running. Voices.

It had to be men from the village, and there seemed quite a few. What they were doing here at night, he did not know though. But he would be glad to see them and find out what was happening.

He was about to walk forward to meet them as they came up the path, but suddenly Ferla grabbed him by the arm and pulled him toward the trees at the side of the track. He nearly asked her what she was doing, but he noticed how silently she moved. That was his first warning that something was wrong.

The second warning was the accents. These were not men from Dromdruin. He could only hear a word or two clearly as they approached, but there was a distinct manner to the way they spoke. These were men from Faladir, and there were quite a few. More than had ever visited all at once before. More in one group than perhaps had visited during his *whole* lifetime before.

Ferla drew him down into the deepest shadows beneath a cluster of rowans, and he did not resist. There was nothing to fear from men of the city. Quite the opposite. They usually brought money to spend with them. But the stories of gold coins were on his mind, and the words of the farmer from only that morning rang in his head. *Like a fox eyeing off ducks in a tree.* That's how he had described them.

No harm came from being cautious, and he knelt beside Ferla, peering out at the road with her, and waited.

They did not have to wait long. The tramp of booted feet was loud, and then the dim shapes of men in the dark came into view. But they were not just men. They were soldiers.

Each figure that passed wore chainmail armor. It was hard to see, but Faran heard its clink, and he saw the long scabbards of their swords hanging down also, when a glimmer of starlight caught some metal stud or decoration on it.

In the middle of the group strode a man, taller than the others. Haughty he seemed, and his helm gleamed silver-bright in the dark. So too his chainmail, and a dark sash looped over his left shoulder and around his right hip.

Almost, Faran thought he was one of the famed Kingshield Knights, but it could not be so. Though they wore silvered armor, their sashes were white. At least, so the stories said.

The tall man did not speak like the others as he walked, but his head turned toward the side of the road and scanned, just for a moment, the shadows beneath the rowans.

Faran felt a shiver of fear run up his spine. He could not see the man's face, and he did not want to. There was something uncanny about him. Something that spoke of danger. And it was more than just the cold professionalism of him, studying the land for signs of life just as a wild animal would before it ventured forth. But not any wild animal. A predator.

The group of warriors passed. There were perhaps twenty, but Faran wondered if that was all of them. Were there more yet to come? Had others ventured down different paths? There were certainly several others at the bottom of the valley. But he knew this was fear prompting his thoughts. He could only worry about what he had seen. Yet that was reason enough for concern.

He and Ferla waited for several minutes before emerging again onto the road. Neither of them wanted to run into another group, if there was one.

"What's going on?" Ferla asked.

He had no answer. "They'll tell us when we reach the village."

She did not reply to that, and he did not blame her.

They paused only long enough then for him to string his bow, and then they set off again. Only this time they did not run. Chance had prevented them from hurrying headlong into the warriors last time. Chance, and Ferla's sharp hearing, but that could not be relied upon again.

They walked, albeit swiftly, and they did not speak. It was as though they were on a hunt, which they had done together many times before, but for all that, he felt vulnerable as though this time he was not really the hunter but the prey.

The forest was silent all around them once more. It seemed to be brooding, as though waiting for a storm to break.

Faran did not like it. Still less did he like it when Ferla whispered in his ear.

"Do you smell it?"

For a moment, he did not know what she meant. But then he smelled it too.

"Smoke," he answered.

They went ahead, but even more slowly now. The smoke grew strong quickly, and they were closing in on the village.

The path widened, for it was more used here. To their left, the faint murmur of the stream came to them. Drom Hairn, it was called. Faran knew it well, and loved it, but this night he wished it were silent. It made it hard for him to hear anything that might be ahead.

Time passed slowly. Unease grew in him such as he had never felt before. It was cold, heart-thumping fear, and it turned his feet to lead.

Ferla must have felt it too. She walked close to him, her shoulder brushing his, and whenever he caught a dim view of her face it was white as winter snow.

The air was very still. It reeked now of smoke, for no breeze dispersed it.

Eventually, the trees thinned and they knew the village was very close. There was no noise, and that too was unusual. There should be singing, or a dog barking, or *something*.

The path led them to open ground, and the village was in sight. It was dim, and nothing moved. No light of candle or lantern shone in any window. But there *was* light. It came from three fires, for three cottages burned.

The fires had died down now. The structures had fallen, and the smaller timbers had already turned to charcoal and ash. Only the larger beams still burned.

"They're not side by side," Ferla said quietly.

He knew what she meant. Had it been a natural fire that spread, it would have moved to the closest cottages. But the three that burned were well separated.

"Someone lit them," he replied. "Deliberately."

It was impossible to believe. It was so far out of the expectation of his day-to-day life that he could not comprehend it. Still less the other horrors that he soon found.

Moving into the village he saw the bodies of the weaver and his wife. They lay on the threshold of their cottage. The weaver had been stabbed several times, and his wife's head rested at a crooked angle. He did not look closely at the wide gash in her neck, but he could not avoid seeing the pool of blood spread out on the ground beside her.

On the other side of the road was the smithy. Herna lay outside it. A large man, and strong. He at least had not been taken by surprise. His mighty hammer had fallen near his hand, and a score of wounds mutilated his body. The earth about him was torn up and trampled. He had fought hard. Perhaps hard enough to kill some of his attackers, for there was blood in several places, and it seemed too much for it all to belong to him.

Had the attackers taken their dead away with them? If so, why? Was it to ensure no one could identify them?

Faran did not want to think about such things, but trying to find the answers kept his mind occupied. If he allowed himself to be overcome by emotion, he would collapse where he was. These were people he had known all his life. Day after day, and year after year they had been there. They were certainties in his life like day and night and summer and winter.

Now they were dead. He would never hear their voices again. They lay still and empty of life like a fallen tree in the forest. Toppled and destroyed.

Ferla vomited, and he reached out and laid a hand on her shoulder. It seemed such a futile gesture. Everything seemed futile to him just now, and it was all he could do not to sick up as well. All that stopped him was a slow anger beginning to burn. These deaths were no accident. The people gone should not be mourned. No. These people had been murdered, and their deaths required vengeance.

Ferla straightened. She did not look at him, perhaps ashamed of her weakness. But he felt guilty that he had controlled his emotions.

They moved ahead, and his cold anger grew.

Everywhere they looked, it was the same. Dead bodies. The young and the old. Blood spattered the ground. Blood spattered cottage walls. Sightless eyes stared at the living as the two of them walked through a path of destruction and murder.

One man had been decapitated. His head had rolled away, face down on the ground. His body lay chest up, his fingers twisted into the dirt.

They passed one of the burning cottages. There were no bodies outside, but inside the smoking ruin were the blackened remains of a family, huddled together. They had barred the door to intruders, but fire had achieved what steel could not.

Faran's anger engulfed him. It roared inside his mind like the fire that had burned here, but it was cold, colder than death itself. He had seen what should never be seen, and he would never be the same again.

Everyone was dead. All their hopes and dreams ashes on the wind.

"Who would do such a thing?" Ferla whispered. "Why would they do it?"

What answers he could give to that, Faran did not know. Nor did he have a chance to think on it.

Ahead, there was movement on the road. A figure came up the path from the other side of the village. Whoever it was took long strides, and they towered above the debris of bodies in the street.

The figure was robed and cowled, and a sense of great power emanated from it.

Ferla hissed, but whether in fear or hatred Faran could not tell. And the figure heard her. It came to a sudden stop. But even as it did so it raised a long and bony arm straight at them.

It was too late to hide this time. They had been seen, and both of them drew arrows from their quivers and nocked them.

2. The King's Men

Slowly, the figure lowered its arm. It was then that Faran realized it was not an arm, but a staff. It was hard to see in the night shadows and shifting light of the fires. He thought too that the figure had shrunk.

But there was no doubt that it took several careful steps toward them. In doing so, it came into a patch of wavery light and Faran saw it more clearly.

"Put down your bows," the figure commanded.

Faran knew that voice. It was the wandering healer who journeyed the lands about dispensing cures in exchange for a barn to sleep in or a meal. His cures were good too, but he was no figure of power. That had been fear and darkness tricking his eyes. He was an old man, poor but kindly.

Faran lowered his bow. Ferla hesitated a moment longer, but she would not know the healer as well as he did. The man had spent a lot of time with his grandfather as he ailed and died. Faran had got to know him fairly well.

"It's been a while, Nuatha. You've been missed these last few years, but you're too late to heal anybody now."

The old man studied him. "Yes, I'm late. Too late to prevent this, but perhaps something can still be saved."

Faran wondered why the man had thought that he could do anything to prevent what had happened here. One extra old man with a staff would have died just as quickly as everyone else.

"There's no one left to save," Faran answered. "Not at this end of the village. Is it any different back there?"

Faran gestured behind the healer in the direction that he had come from.

The old man frowned, as though misunderstanding what had been said. Then he shook his head.

"No. There's nobody alive back there either. There would not be."

Faran did not know what the healer meant by that, but just then a dog barked somewhere close by in the dark and the old man spun to face the sound, his staff held high and his brown robes twisting about him. For a moment, he gave off that sense of power again, but then he lowered his staff. His hood had fallen off, revealing his silver-white hair. Suddenly, he seemed even older and frailer than he had ever seemed before.

"You move fast, for an old man," Ferla said.

"Traveling keeps me young," the healer answered. "The open road would be a dangerous place otherwise."

Faran was about to say that villages were no safer, but he thought better of it. Dromdruin had always been a safe place. Until now.

"We have to get word of this to the king," he said instead.

There was a crash behind them, and sparks flew up into the air. One of the few remaining structural beams of a burning cottage had collapsed.

Nuatha glanced at it, and then fixed Faran with his bright gaze. However old he was, those eyes always seemed to pierce whatever he looked at.

"Think, Faran. Think."

"What is there to think about? We have to get word to the king. He needs to know what happened so he can chase down whoever did this and bring them to justice."

Nuatha slowly shook his head. "The king already knows, Faran. Who do you think sent these men? This is not the work of robbers. It was done by warriors, or those who call themselves that. And there must have been a number of them to overpower even a small village like this. People don't die easily."

Faran could not believe what he was hearing. "You can't be serious. The king *knows*?"

"He knows. He will have ordered it. And those who carried out his instructions are the king's own men. Warriors he trusts."

Faran stood there, speechless. He could not believe that.

Ferla spoke quietly. "You must be mistaken."

"Anything is possible, lass. I've lived a long time. I've been mistaken many times. But this is not one of them. We have to leave here, and now. We're in danger. Grave danger."

"Whoever did this," Faran said, still unwilling to even think the king could be behind it, "has gone. We saw them a good way back on the road."

"You *saw* them? And they didn't attack you?"

"We saw them, but they didn't see us," Ferla told him. "We were hiding."

"Just as well for you. Or you'd both be corpses now. But that's something they'll soon try to remedy. At least, when they discover their mistake."

"What mistake?" Faran asked.

It seemed that Nuatha was going to say one thing, but he said another at the last moment.

"That anyone from this village remains alive. Anyone at all."

That did not make much sense to Faran. "They've been and gone. They'll not likely come back. We should be safe here now, and we need to start digging graves."

Nuatha leaned on his staff, and his eyes were not unkindly. But when he spoke, it was with force.

"You don't understand, Faran. You're not safe here. You may never be safe again. The warriors have … ways and means of learning things. Or their leader does. They'll soon learn their mistake. They'll soon learn that you remain alive, and they'll return to fix that. Best we're not here when that happens."

Faran did not understand any of this. He could not even fathom that his village had been attacked. But he knew he had not been thinking clearly since he discovered that. He was in shock, and he was only just beginning to realize it.

He glanced at Ferla. So often, he took his lead from her, but she said nothing and merely looked at the healer as though he were a puzzle she had not yet worked out.

Nuatha straightened. "Come. Follow me if you value your lives. I'll protect you."

The healer strode away then. One moment he had been leaning on his staff like a weary old man, and the next he seemed filled with energy and purpose. He was not like any other old man Faran had ever met.

With a quick glance at each other, Faran and Ferla followed him.

Nuatha did not look back. He either did not care if they followed, or he was a man used to being obeyed. Faran knew it was not the first. His grandfather had been a man of good judgement, and he had held the healer in the highest of esteem. Almost, it seemed at times, that he revered him. But it could not be the second either. The man was a wandering healer. A vagabond. And while respected wherever he went because of his skill, he was little more than a beggar.

The old man walked briskly for all his age. He slipped between two cottages and moved off the road and headed toward the forest. That at least, if nothing else, made sense.

But so much else did not. For what possible reason would the king send men to destroy Dromdruin village? There was no reason at all for such a thing. And how on earth did the old man think he could protect them?

3. Into Darkness

Nuatha had taken charge, and Faran was grateful for that. He needed time to think, and time to understand what was happening.

He glanced at Ferla. She did not speak to him as they followed the healer, but an understanding passed between them. For now, they must stay alive. Later, they could work out what was happening.

They came to the edge of the village. The forest loomed ahead of them, dark and forbidding. But not as dark as what lay behind. The two of them turned and took one last look at what had become of their home. A graveyard. The site of a hideous evil. Their childhood memories entwined now through a vision of horror.

A moment they stood together, and then as one they turned and followed the healer into the darkness.

And dark it was. The night was growing old now, and the trees here were thick. They grew near the river, and the soil was fertile because of the flooding of ages past. But this was Faran's home too. He was not scared of the dark, but he did admit to himself that he was scared of what might be in it. The tall warrior that he had seen, and the way he had looked around him and seemed to own the very road he trod, was one such thing that he would not want to meet. Perhaps there were others. But even the band of warriors with that man seemed insignificant now. Better to meet all of them together than their leader by himself.

Nuatha led without hesitation. It had been years since last he was here, but the old man seemed sure of where he was going. That was not really surprising. He had lived here on and off and would know the paths well. But Faran was not sure where he intended to go. The way he led them was now downslope and toward the creek itself.

The inclination of the land grew swiftly, and soon they were clambering down a bank. The slap of water against stones and the gurgle of it as it rushed ahead became loud.

Nuatha did not hesitate when he came to the water. He walked in, until he was knee deep, and then slowly worked his way upstream.

Faran glanced at Ferla. He saw a flicker of fear in her eyes, for she understood as well as he what this meant. The old man feared pursuit. He feared that dogs might be loosed to track them, and this was to hide their trail. If not, then at least it would make it harder for any tracker when daylight came.

The two of them steadied each other, and waded in after the healer.

Once again, they struggled to keep up with him. He moved ahead with some speed and a lot of agility. It was not easy because the water flowed fairly fast, and they were now midstream.

It was cold and uncomfortable. They would not get dry again until the sun came up tomorrow, but Faran did not really mind. If the healer feared pursuit, perhaps he was right to do so. And this was a good way of throwing it off. Still, hiding trails in the wild was not the sort of skill Faran expected the healer to possess. It seemed there was more to him than Faran knew, and he suddenly wished he could speak to his grandfather and discover what he had known about the old man.

Nuatha led them a long way upstream. Farther than Faran would have gone, but perhaps that was just as well. The thought of being pursued by dogs was unnerving. Then again, if the warriors had dogs, he would have seen them on the road. More likely, he and Ferla would have been discovered by them as they lay in hiding. But had they seen all the warriors? It was possible there had been another group, or even more, on different paths.

Overall, Faran was glad the healer was so cautious, but after some half an hour he began to move across to the other side of the creek and then up onto the bank. Faran noticed that he chose a place that was grassed rather than bare sand or dirt. That would help hide their trail too.

They came up onto the bank, dripping wet from the waist down. A massive mulberry tree grew there. Faran knew it. Here, he had enjoyed its fruits later in the season many times. He could not see them now because of the dark, but they would still be hard and green.

They were still below its arched boughs when they saw the fox. They had somehow managed to surprise it, which was a rare occurrence with foxes. But surprised or not, it gave them a quick glance and trotted away into the dark, wary but unhurried.

"It has a den near here," Ferla whispered.

Nuatha leaned on his staff and looked at them. "We need food," he said quietly. "There's a farm cottage ahead. We'll risk venturing inside and scrounging what supplies we can get. But walk carefully, and be prepared to run."

"You speak as though the farmer is dead," Faran said. "But this is quite a way from the village."

The old man gave a slight shrug. "If he's alive, and his family with him, we'll give them warning and tell them to flee. But the enemy will not have left witnesses. Not even this far away."

He turned and walked away again, before they had a chance to ask any more questions. And Faran had a new one added to his list. Who exactly were the enemy? The old man had said it with bitterness in his voice, as though he had encountered them previously. As though there was some *history* between them.

But they followed him as before, moving up a sandy trail. Here, they had no choice but to leave tracks behind them. The trees were too thick to either side to walk off the path.

The trail leveled out and the trees gave way to an open field. Faran had been here many times. It was an oat paddock, although just now the green shoots were little more than ankle high. It attracted hares though, and the hares in turn attracted foxes.

They moved through various fields, each separated by wicker fencing, and came to the last before the farmer's cottage. Dardenath was his name, though Faran had rarely seen him. He did not come into the village often, but his wife and son did. They sold meat, and in the field around the cottage grazed the white cattle with black ears and noses that were common in the valley.

The cattle were not bedded down though. Nor were they grazing. They were in a far corner of the paddock, and they lowed occasionally as though something disturbed them. What that might be, Faran did not know. It was too dark to see anything.

The cottage stood in the night shadows. It, at least, was not set to fire. But nor were there lights within it. If the farmer and his family were alive, they had not seen the smoke in the village. That was hard to believe. Or perhaps they had gone to help, and had never come back. That seemed more likely.

But one thing was certain. They were not here now, for the front door stood ajar. Or if they were, they were dead.

Nuatha took the lead as he had from the beginning. But he did not hurry here. He took his time, circling the house first and coming round to the front door again.

He glanced at Faran and Ferla, as if assessing their readiness. But he seemed pleased when he saw that each of them had nocked arrows to their bows.

The healer pushed the door all the way open with his staff. It creaked a little as it opened, but not much. And there the healer stood. A long while he waited before he stepped forward again, the staff held high before him as though he could use it as a weapon. For the first time, Faran wondered if he could. The healer seemed capable for an old man. More than capable.

They followed him into the room. It was a simple space, with a large table in the middle. This had been overturned. To the left was a kitchen, but the fire in the hearth was dead.

There was no sign of Dardenath or his family. But there were two doors in the far wall. They would lead to the bedrooms.

Nuatha opened them one by one and looked inside.

"Nothing," he said. "There's no sign of anyone. But we're not safe here. Hurry, and collect whatever food is available."

They moved to the kitchen. There were sausages hanging from the rafters, cured by smoke from the cooking carried out close by. They would last, and Faran and Ferla collected them quickly. There were several hams too, but these were too bulky, though they did cut off several thick slices.

"Get the cheeses also," Nuatha said. Then he moved to the front door and kept watch.

There were both soft cheeses and hard, but Faran and Ferla took only the hard ones. They would last much longer, and they were more nutritious as well. The soft cheeses contained a lot of water.

On the table they found a loaf of bread also. It was heavy and dark, of the kind often favored in Dromdruin.

It was a day old, but it would last some while and they took it too.

They each had a small hunter's satchel, looped sideways across their shoulders. This was useful out on a hunt, just as much for taking food with them as bringing back butchered game or foraged roots, tubers and herbs. They filled them now with their new supplies, and then rejoined Nuatha near the door.

The night was dark, but Faran wanted to be out there. Field and wood were his home now, and he did not wish to see cottages and paths again. How could he ever look at buildings and not see dead bodies within them? Even if only the memory of them.

But what if they were wrong about this farm? What if Dardenath returned? He would need the food that had been taken.

"Do you really think the farmer is dead?" he asked Nuatha.

The healer did not take his eyes away from their study of the night-shadowed fields.

"He's not likely alive. Neither him nor his family. I'm sorry."

Faran knew with a sinking feeling that this was probably right.

"I still don't understand. Why would the king's men kill them? Why would they kill *everyone*?"

Nuatha pulled up the brown hood over his head. "It's time to go," was his only answer.

The healer stepped out into the night, his strides quick but his head turning slightly side to side so as not to miss anything. For just a moment he reminded Faran of the tall man on the road in armor.

Ferla followed the figure, and Faran followed her. He did not yet have any answers to his questions, and he did not like it. But he liked less remaining in that cottage.

He thought of his own cottage. He had not seen it at the village, for it was at the far end that they had not reached. It, too, would be standing empty as did this one. Would anyone ever live there again?

With grief in his heart, he followed the healer into the night. The old man headed straight for the closest hedge. Obviously, he did not trust the night alone to hide them, and that was probably wise. Dark as it was, movement could still be seen out in the open.

Clouds scudded across the sky here and there, and the temperature dropped. It felt even cooler than it was, for their clothes were still wet from the creek. What they needed now was rest and a fire, but they were the two things they could not have.

They moved on through the night, three silent shadows, grim and furtive. And they moved quickly for the most part, for the healer led them at a startling pace. Yet at whiles he was still too, standing motionless and staring into the darkness ahead as though he could penetrate it with his mind even if his eyes had failed.

So they continued, and Faran felt exhaustion begin to grip him. When would this night end? He had been on the move since dawn yesterday, and he had walked endless miles. He could not go on much farther, but he could not let the old man shame him. If the healer felt the same tiredness, he did not show any sign of it.

It was some time well after midnight when they stood upon a ridge and looked down at Dromdruin valley. Faran could no longer smell smoke, and had not for hours. Nor could he see any fire where the village lay. It would have burned out now. All he saw instead was a vast blackness, and fear gripped him.

It seemed to him that the stars swam in the sky, and a terrible urge to run came over him. He did not know what he was scared of, but suddenly he knew that death was close and his only chance was to flee.

But he resisted that urge. He looked at Ferla, and she was white in the face. She felt it too.

The healer did not look down into the valley. His gaze was cast upward into the sky, and then suddenly he grabbed them by the shoulders and hauled them down into some bushes beneath the nearest tree.

"Be still!" he hissed. "And make no noise!"

4. Time for Answers

Faran looked up, following the gaze of the old man, and he wished that he had not.

Something blotted out the stars. Vast it seemed, and evil. Yet it moved with grace. And a hunter's intent. Suddenly the words of the village drunkard came back to him, and he knew the man had told the truth. *A bat I saw, gliding silently over the village green. A bat, big as a man, and fear enough filled the sky to sober ten drunk men. I swear it.*

Faran could swear it too now, and he was not drunk.

The creature swept in from the south, and it banked and turned above them. It glided on the dark wings of a bat, but it was no cumbrous and slow-moving animal; it was a hunter of the air, and its every move spoke of grace and death.

There was no sound. Not of leathery wings, but even as it passed above them, and there was a glimpse of a pale body, it screamed. The sound was like a woman, as though a human voice had given vent to unspeakable pain. It slid into Faran's ears like twin knives, and his heart pounded in his chest.

The urge to run then was overwhelming. He had to get away. And yet he knew too that to move was to be seen, and the two opposing forces gripped him. He shook all over, and he felt Ferla beside him tremble.

Nuatha remained as he was. Like a man carved of stone, he knelt beneath the foliage and did not move. Only his eyes shifted, tracking the flight of the creature with sharp focus, but not a trace of fear.

If the old man could be so calm, Faran could match it. He stilled his trembling, and suppressed the urge to run. He too watched the creature now, aiming for Nuatha's seeming detachment. He even achieved some measure of it, but it had become easier. With some graceful strokes of those leathery wings, the thing moved well away from them.

The creature faded from sight quickly, swallowed by the dark to which it belonged. But they did not move. Instead, they remained huddled where they were, deep in the shadows.

The bat thing did not return, but they heard its terrible cry twice more, far away over Dromdruin valley somewhere. It came to them from a great distance, shrill and high-pitched. And only a little less terrible for the faintness of it.

Eventually, the feeling of dread passed, and Nuatha stood, using his staff to lever himself up.

"A close call," he said. "And you both did well. The desire to flee such dread has killed many. That's the purpose of the creature's cry. To draw prey from hiding and make it flee so that it can be hunted. But you resisted well."

"It *was* hunting, wasn't it?" Faran asked. "It was hunting us."

How he knew that, he was not sure. But he felt it in his bones with a certainty that chilled him.

"It was certainly hunting," the old man answered. "But whether for you or for me, I'm not sure. Either way, all the more reason to get far from this place, and quickly."

"What was it though?" Ferla asked.

The healer looked away into the night. "You know your stories, lass. Bedtime stories to some – but waking nightmares to others."

Ferla seemed to repress a shudder. "Of old, there were said to be creatures like that. But they were killed when the city of Faladir was founded."

"Killed? Yes, they were killed. King Conduil was a great man, and he won many victories. But none of them were complete. The evils of the world were diminished, but not destroyed. In dark places they hid. And long they dwelled in secret. But they haunt the skies once more, and walk the land also."

The old man looked as if he would say no more, but then he surprised them, offering more than he had so far on this long, long night.

"What you just saw was once called an elù-drak. It is a creature of the dark. It is a thing of ultimate evil, long banished, but now, it seems, drawn back by a greater evil still. Perhaps even invited. There are many such creatures left over from the elù-haraken, the Shadowed Wars of old."

"What's it doing *here*?" Faran asked.

"No doubt it was involved in the destruction of your village. More likely in scouting things out than fighting. There were men brought here for that, less dangerous maybe, but dangerous enough. Although he who leads them is more dangerous now than the elù-drak, perhaps."

"And who is that?"

The old man grunted. "I've told you enough for now. That much you have a right to know. But more must wait. We're not out of danger yet, and there'll be time enough for talk when we're safe."

The old man moved off into the night, and after a quick glance at Ferla, Faran and she followed. The healer, it seemed, had some of the answers to what was going on. And he was right about the danger too. Faran did not feel safe yet. Not with that thing hunting the skies.

Nuatha led them through the wilderness. He seemed to know where he was going, even if that meant through the deepest and thickest woods and the roughest terrain. A few hours ago, Faran would have put that down to a poor choice of path, and a lack of knowledge of the countryside. But he had learned better swiftly. The old man knew where he was at all times, and his choice of route was no accident. It was to help hide them, both from pursuit over ground, and now it seemed, in the skies. The healer could do things, and knew things, that Faran would never have expected.

He cast his mind back over all that he knew of the old man, but it wasn't much. His grandfather had known him well, but never spoke of him much. In retrospect, that seemed strange.

Faran stumbled slightly as he walked. He realized something else, too. The healer had been forthcoming just before, but he had deftly avoided answering the question of who had led the band of warriors, and who, it seemed, also controlled the elù-drak. And for that matter, how did the old man even know what name to put to that creature in the sky?

They kept moving through what remained of the night, and they kept a watch behind them for signs of pursuit. The sky was harder to observe, but whenever they came out into the open they did so warily and with many an upward glance.

But they saw nothing untoward, either behind or above. It was something to be grateful for, because increasingly Faran began to think that they really were being hunted. That thing in the sky was no accident. It had been looking for something. Prey maybe, but perhaps a specific quarry.

If the man who controlled it, that tall man with a silver helm, knew someone had escaped the massacre of the village he would certainly act to fix that mistake. He had the look about him of one who relentlessly carried out orders, and left no loose ends behind him. He would crush a loose end as an ordinary man would tread an ant, and feel less emotion about it.

Faran did not like to think that way. He did not like to judge people until he knew them well, but in this case that one glance through the night shadows seemed enough. The man had sent a chill up his spine.

There was no way for him to know if anyone had escaped the village though. As long as they were not seen, then perhaps the three of them had eluded notice. But the way the healer spoke, and by the way he acted, that seemed still in question. And it was clear the old man had a better idea of what was going on and why than he had so far said.

Faran was surprised when it happened, for the night had seemed endless, but at last the night-time shadows turned to hues of gray, the stars faded in the sky and the eastern horizon glowed with light from the yet unrisen sun.

But soon after, the sun did rise. Dawn broke across the land and the three travelers reached the end of their endurance. At least, two of them did.

Nuatha glanced at them, his bright blue eyes taking them in at a glance and measuring them as though assessing if they had any spark left to walk another hundred feet.

Apparently, he thought not, for he called a halt within a little oak wood. "Time to rest," he said. "But no fire."

They sat down and ate some of the ham they had taken from the farmer's cottage. It was smoky and salty, just the way that Faran liked it.

When they were done though, Faran looked at the healer and for all his tiredness a determination gripped him.

"It's time for some answers, Nuatha. Why would those soldiers do what they did at the village? Why can we not get help from the king? And how did you know what that creature in the sky was?"

5. The Kingshield Knights

Nuatha did not answer at once. He sat there, his knees drawn up and his staff resting upon them.

"Good questions, all." he replied. "And what of you, Ferla? What would you like to know?"

"Why was everyone killed?"

The old man nodded slowly. "I'll answer as best I can. But the situation is complicated, and even I don't know all of what is happening."

He looked away from them for a moment, as though gathering his thoughts.

"All of this began long ago. If there is ever a true beginning to anything. You know, of course, the tale of the founding of Faladir?"

"We know what everyone knows of that," Faran said. "There was a great war, and the creatures of the dark were defeated by King Conduil. But that was long ago, and is mostly legend. What has that got to do with last night?"

"Patience, lad. Did you not just last night see a legend itself? You saw one of the elù-drak, which few have ever seen – and survived to remember."

It was true, and Faran bit his lip. At least the old man was talking. He could let him tell what he knew at his own pace.

The healer continued. "Of old, there were many creatures such as the elù-drak. King Conduil was a great man, and he won a battle against them. And at that time, he also established the Kingshield Knights." He turned his gaze to Faran. "So they come from the time of legends too, but you know the truth of their existence better than most."

Faran nodded. His grandfather had been one, for a time.

"And what was their one true purpose, Faran?"

"To guard the Morleth Stone taken from the enemy. It could not be destroyed, but they swore oaths to guard it, and keep it from those who would seek it out and use it."

"Very good. You know the history of the Kingshield Knights. As you should. But what of them now?"

Faran was surprised at the question. "Everyone knows about them. Nothing has changed. They still guard the stone and they wander the land, bringing peace, wisdom and justice with them."

The old man sighed. "That is what they have long done. For a very, very long time. But who leads them now?"

"The king himself is the First Knight now. Even as the first king was in the days of old."

"Indeed. And why did your grandfather leave the order of knights? A thing not said to have happened before in all the long history of the knights?"

"He said the king was a pompous ass. And a fool."

Ferla seemed shocked. "Faran! You can't say that."

"I'm just repeating what my grandfather said. And he would have known."

Nuatha grinned. "Your grandfather was a brave man. But he paid for it. Still, he was a wise man also. The king *was* a pompous ass, and worse. He was a man of great pride, and in his youth he had enormous physical and mental prowess. He outstripped the other knights, by far. But still, pride was his weakness."

Faran thought of the last years of his grandfather's life. The king had stripped him of estates and lands, and the old man had died in poverty. But not once had he ever said that he regretted speaking his mind.

Nuatha leaned forward. "Do you see where this is going, Faran?"

Faran shook his head. He did not know.

Ferla leaned forward though. "It was his pride. He has done what should not be done, hasn't he?"

The healer looked grave. "Yes he has. He was strong, in body and in mind, except for his one weakness. But that was how the stone got to him. Through his pride."

Faran understood now, as unthinkable as it was. "The king has *used* the stone?"

"He has. But now the stone uses him. And evil is loosed upon the land."

Faran let out a long breath. Every tale he had ever heard, every legend, warned against this. The Morleth Stone must be guarded, but never used. It was ultimate evil, and when it was used the knights would fall from their high position and the realm would be driven to peril such as it had not known since the chaos of the Shadowed Wars.

"So that was why Dromdruin was destroyed? Is this happening all over the realm?"

Nuatha pursed his lips, thinking on what answer to give.

"I've only just returned here from traveling far away. I cannot be sure what is happening in the rest of the realm. But I have heard rumors. Evil is abroad. Dark things stir. There is unrest in the city, though no one seems to know what lies behind it. But as for Dromdruin – no, I cannot say that I have heard of other villages being attacked."

Faran considered that. Things were beginning to make some sort of sense now. And he remembered other things his grandfather had said about the king. A dangerous man, he had called him.

Yet still, it made no sense for Dromdruin to be singled out.

"Why my village then? Why attack it, and not others? Does it have something to do with my grandfather?"

Nuatha frowned. "I haven't considered that before, but yes, in a roundabout way it just might."

"You don't sound very sure," Ferla said.

The old man shrugged, but did not answer.

Faran was thinking quickly though. What had made the old man return here when he has not been here for years? And why had he been so friendly with his grandfather?

"How do you know all this, Nuatha? Where does a wandering healer learn of the doings of kings? And everything else you seem to know."

The old man rolled his staff backward and forward over his knee.

"I get around, Faran. Like you say, I'm a wanderer. I hear things. I learn things. I figure things out."

"But how—"

"That's enough for now. I don't know about you, but I'm deadly tired. We need rest. Time to sleep, lad. Time to sleep."

Faran was not going to be put off though, even if it was all he could do to keep his eyes open.

"Why did they attack Dromdruin? Tell me that, if you know."

The old man looked at him hard, but he answered after a pause.

"Your grandfather was stubborn too, so I guess I shouldn't be surprised. This much is obvious. They killed the entire village because they guessed, or knew, some kind of a threat existed there. But obviously, they weren't sure who it was. Otherwise they would have probably killed that person alone."

The old man lay down on the ground then, but he spoke over his shoulder.

"Now sleep, Faran. You need rest. And if you don't, I do."

There was not much to do or say after that. Faran glanced at Ferla, but she merely shrugged as if to say that the healer was right.

But he could tell she wanted to know more too. Her green eyes glanced back to where the old man lay, and there was speculation in them. Then she too lay down, her bright red hair spilling out of the hood.

Faran lay back as well. The morning sun was warm and bright. The sky was blue. He felt drowsy as he rarely had before, but when he closed his eyes he saw things that he did not wish to.

Blood and death and injustice snaked through his thoughts. He could not sleep, but he could not stay awake either. He drifted in and out of wakefulness, and he tossed and turned finding no position comfortable.

So the hours passed. And strangely, every time Faran turned he caught a glimpse of the old man. He was not lying down anymore. He sat there, as he had before, with the staff resting on his knees, and he was motionless as a statue. But still, those penetrating eyes seemed to take everything in as they always did.

Was he keeping guard? Faran thought he might be. And it was probably just as well. Someone needed to. It was possible soldiers followed their trail, but unlikely. More of a worry was the elù-drak. But they were well hidden where they were in the wood. Even so, he was glad that someone had the strength to keep awake.

The old man was surprising. He was the first to lie down, but he could barely have slept at all. Maybe it was true what people said. The elderly needed little in the way of sleep.

Maybe. But it was still surprising. That old man had outwalked he and Ferla through the night. Had he wished to, Faran was sure he could have kept going this morning. He had only stopped for his two companions.

He was a strange old man, and stronger than he looked. Back in the village when they had first met in the dark, he had been a figure of power if only for a few moments. Unless it was just the shadows and smoke playing tricks.

Faran turned yet again and finally drifted into a troubled sleep.

6. Like a Warrior

The sun was high in the sky when Faran woke, and he had slept deeply, if only for a little while. He felt strange and groggy, and the sleep had not quite refreshed him.

He sat up and looked around. Of the healer, there was no sign at all, but Ferla was already sitting up, looking at him.

"Where's Nuatha?" he asked.

She shrugged. "He was gone when I woke a little while ago."

"Gone? Do you think he's abandoned us?"

"You know him better than I do. But it seems unlikely to me. He doesn't strike me as that sort of man. But who knows?"

Faran could not clear the fog from his mind. "I wouldn't have thought so either. But maybe he thought better of joining up with us. Who could blame him, really?"

She ran a hand through her long red hair, teasing it out as though she were teasing out thoughts from her mind.

"I wouldn't blame him. He might be safer away from us. But one thing is for sure, we're safer with him."

"Do you really think so?"

"I know it. And so do you. If not for him, we might have stayed in the village. If we had, we might be dead, lying alongside all those other bodies."

What she said was true. But it wasn't something he wanted to think about.

"Then there was that elù-drak," she continued. "He pulled us in to cover just in time to save us there, too. Without him, we would have been seen."

"That might have just been luck," he answered.

Her eyebrows rose, red-hued like her hair. "You don't believe that."

In truth, he did not. The old man was more than he seemed. But he was not here now, whatever he had done yesterday.

"One thing is certain," he said. "With him or without him, at least the two of us have to stick together."

She looked him straight in the eye, but he could not tell what she was thinking.

"We're all that's left," she said eventually. "We're all who remember what once was. That was taken from us, but we still have each other. I'm not going anywhere without you."

He suddenly felt close to her then. Very close, as he sometimes did. But it was stronger now than it had ever been.

"I'll not go anywhere without you, either."

She looked at him a moment, and then she cast her gaze to the woods around them. Immediately, her hand reached out for the bow lying beside her.

Faran scrambled up, snatching his bow as he rose. But it was only Nuatha.

The healer stood not far away. For just a moment a shaft of sunlight caught his old brown robes, and they seemed to glimmer white, but then he moved toward them and the bright light was gone.

Faran cursed himself silently. He was a hunter, used to the wild and alert to its ways. How had the old man walked through the woods and approached without him noticing?

But just as well it was only the healer. It could have been one of those soldiers. Or something else. Faran cursed again.

"I think," Nuatha said, walking into their little camp, "that we'll all stick together for a while."

"Where have you been?" Faran asked.

"Here and there," the old man replied. "Someone had to have a look around, and see if we're being followed."

"And what did you find?"

"Nothing that I shouldn't, which is just as well for us. The pursuit hasn't begun yet, or it's well back. You two have had more luck than you know."

Faran knew those were true words. But he did not feel lucky. Not with everything that he once knew destroyed, and everyone that he used to know murdered. But he and Ferla were alive, so he could not dispute what the healer said.

"If there's no sign of anyone, why don't we rest here a few more hours. We can move again at night, when it'll be easier to hide anyway."

The healer drew his old robes about him, and Faran wondered how he could ever have mistaken them for being white.

"I don't think so. There are still a few hours of daylight left, and we can travel many miles. Better to do that, and put more distance between us and Dromdruin. Then we can rest the night."

Faran did not like the way the healer just assumed that he was in charge, though he had never quite said anything like it.

"If there's no sign of anyone, what's the hurry to move now?"

Nuatha gazed at him, his expression unreadable.

"This is going to be a long journey if you insist on doing the opposite of everything I suggest. But I'll tell you something you obviously haven't thought through. The enemy may not be close, but that doesn't mean you've escaped. Not by a long way. And you've forgotten the elùdrak. It's a creature of the night. It can fly long and far, and it sees well. You're not beyond its reach yet, and you don't want to see it again if you can help it. Better by far for us to move through the day when it rests, and stay still and concealed at night when it hunts. Is there anything wrong with my logic?"

Faran nearly spoke several times. He wanted to dispute what the healer said. But he couldn't.

"Fine," he muttered. "You're correct."

He knew the old man was, and he certainly knew that he had no wish to see that *thing* in the sky again. None at all. But he had not known that it rested during the day.

"Let's go then," Nuatha said, and he moved away into the woods, just expecting to be followed again.

Faran ground his teeth, but Ferla flashed him a wicked grin. She was enjoying this. Usually, she liked to put him in his place, but it seemed that she liked the healer doing it almost as much.

They moved off after the old man, and Faran pulled up his hood despite the warm sun. He had no wish to talk just at the moment, but Ferla only grinned all the harder. But it did not last. Her humor faded quickly. No doubt her mind had slipped back to the horrors that she had seen the previous night.

The healer moved with great caution, as he always did. He never took them along a path that would reveal them in the open on a ridge. He followed the low ways, and moved from wood to wood and thicket to thicket, wary as a deer.

Faran grew to respect that, for the old man seemed to move by some instinct that was quick and sure. If Faran had to choose the route himself, he could have done no better. But certainly it would have taken him longer. He would have had to stop and think. Even though he had been hunting for years and was skilled. Even if he knew how to avoid being seen and even smelled by prey. It was impressive what the healer could do, but Faran could not help but wonder where he had acquired the skill. Had he been a hunter himself in his youth, before he learned the healing arts?

Nuatha kept them going even as the sun began to drop toward the rim of the world. They followed a high ridge now, but the old man stuck to the trees that grew on the eastern side, for this provided not only cover because of the vegetation but additional concealment due to the shadows cast from the westering sun and the top of the ridgeline.

But when dusk was turning into evening, he slipped up through a wood and topped the crest, moving down into the trees on the western side.

Night fell, and the healer found another good campsite soon after. A tiny rivulet wound down from the ridge, and a thick stand of pines offered good shelter from rain, wind and hopefully the prying eyes of the elù-drak should it by some chance fly overhead.

They set up a little camp again. This involved no more than putting down their hunter's satchels, their bows and quivers, and heaping some old pine needles together to form beds.

"No fire," Nuatha said again, as he had the previous night.

Faran had also noticed as they traveled that the old man watched their backtrail nearly as much as ahead of them.

"Do you really think someone might pursue us? We're a long way from the village now."

Nuatha sat down on his heap of pine needles. "There's no one following us yet. At least not closely. But there will be."

"How can you be so sure?"

"Best hope I'm wrong, lad."

There it was again. The healer had a habit of never quite answering a question. And he was good at it.

The night grew dark about them quickly. Faran loved the light and warmth that a campfire gave. And there was something comforting about it in the wild. Even so, he did not quibble with what the healer said.

There was unlikely to be another person for many miles to see the light from even a large fire, either soldier or traveler, but the elù-drak would see such a thing. Even if it were a small fire lit only briefly, it might attract the creature from miles away, and that was one thing that he could do without.

When the healer was right, he was right, and so Faran ate his share of the cold meal and put thoughts of hot food aside.

They did not speak. It was not that a camaraderie had failed to grow between them. It had. The old man had made wise choices, and Faran appreciated that. And he had stuck with them too. Had he wished, he could have walked away from them and gone his own way. But eating a cold meal in the dark gave no impetus to conversation.

So it was that they settled down soon after to sleep once more.

Faran was not so tired as he had been, but he was still tired enough. This time, he fell asleep swiftly and descended into a series of dreams that haunted him. A sense of unease lay over his mind, and then something woke him to a feeling of panic.

He sat up and looked around. It must have only been a nightmare, and yet he noticed that Ferla stirred to wakefulness near him, and the old man was standing in the center of the camp, his staff held before him like a warrior ready to fight.

"What's going on?" Faran whispered.

But the healer did not answer. And Faran forgot the question. A strange mist, silvery white, was rising from the ground just beside their camp.

7. Marked for Death

Faran strung his bow swiftly, and the mist swirled up from the ground.

"Beware!" the healer cried, but he made no move to flee, and did not seem agitated.

If the old man was not scared, neither would Faran allow any fear to show.

But that did not mean that he did not feel it.

The mist eddied and then took form. It became a man, and a tall one. In silver armor he stood, both chainmail and helm glittering pale against the night. And from shoulder to hip was looped a crimson sash.

Faran knew him. It was the soldier that he had seen on the road to Dromdruin, and hidden from. He wished he could hide now, but the healer seemed unsurprised and merely leaned on his staff and watched as though this were no more unusual than some forest animal stumbling into their camp.

Faran straightened. He would not be scared. He had a bow, and it might punch through armor. Or if not, he could shoot between helm and chainmail collar.

The figure became startlingly vivid, yet it did not quite seem perfectly solid either. There was still a faint suggestion of mistiness about it.

The man stood there, his pose casual and yet threatening. He seemed a young man, and long hair, raven-black, spilled out from beneath his helm. But his skin, and especially his face, were pallid. The sharp eyes set in that face missed nothing. They glanced around, but it seemed that everything they saw provoked a feeling of disdain, for his lips curled into a faint sneer.

But when he spoke, to Faran's surprise, it was with great courtesy, and even, perhaps, respect.

"Greetings, Nuatha. I believe that is the name you use, at the moment."

"I have many names in many places. That one will do as well as any other."

The knight gave a slight bow of his head, but he never took his gaze off the old man.

"It is more fitting than some, maybe. Especially if you wish to wander around unknown. But did you really think you fooled us these last few decades? We knew who you were, and whither you went."

The healer gave a shrug of immense indifference. "I did not know that the comings and goings of one old man were of import to the high and the noble."

"Oh, but they are. And you know it. You tried to hide from us, and failed. Why can you not acknowledge that?"

The old man lowered his staff, and then leaned against it.

"Because that would give you a fat head, Lindercroft, and your head is already overblown with thoughts of grandness. It always was, but I see your arrogance has grown greater."

The knight laughed, and the sound of it was light and airy, but his dark eyes, dark as his hair, were cold pits of blackness.

"Arrogance? Me? I think not. Greater power has taught me humility. There is so much to know, and so much to do, how could I be anything but humble in the face of that? I have seen the mysteries and the very powers that form and substance the world. That has taught me humility. No. The arrogance is yours. You have come here to stop us. But our glory cannot be brought to an end now. You are too late, and too weak to try."

The old man looked sad. "Glory? Is that what you call it? Look into your heart and see what you have done. You have fallen far, Lindercroft. Far indeed. And it pains me."

The knight laughed. "You mean the village? Ah, spare me your pity, old man. I do not need it. Your age has passed. A new age dawns. If a village must be laid low, what of it? If a farmer needs new land, does he not fell the trees and till the earth? Who mourns a few trees when food is put on people's tables instead? It is the way of the world. You should know that better than anyone."

"I'll not debate with you, Lindercroft."

The misty figure of the knight wavered slightly. "But you will still persist in trying to stop us?"

"I do as I must," Nuatha answered. Faran sensed a deep sadness in the old man's voice, but there was a well of determination there also, and it ran deep.

The figure of the knight straightened, and his hand rested close to the hilt of his great sword.

"Your choice is not unexpected, but you must know by now that our powers are greater than they were. Far greater."

Nuatha slowly shook his head. "You mean the hold of the stone over you is all the stronger. What you can no longer see is that you were greater without it. Once, you were all the best of men."

The knight stirred uneasily, but his voice was sure when he gave answer.

"We remain the best of men. Only, now, we are even better. We have become stronger, wiser and more adept at magic. Shall I show you? Shall I burn you in bright fire until you see the truth?"

The knight raised his hand, but Nuatha merely stood still looking back at him.

Faran had heard enough though, and the old man had helped him. He would not allow him to be threatened or harmed. Not if he could help it.

In one swift motion he nocked an arrow to his bow, drew and loosed it. With a hiss it flew through the air and into the figure of the knight. It hit where he aimed: the slight gap between helm and chainmail collar.

But it seemed that there was nothing of true substance to actually strike. The arrow clattered away into the trees behind the knight, and all that happened to that sinister figure was that the mist of which it was made swirled and eddied where the flight of the arrow had cut through it.

The knight turned to look at him, for Faran stood to one side. The arrogant sneer on his face deepened to a murderous scowl.

"You are of the village and marked for death, boy. You always have been, but now I shall see to it, personally."

Faran was growing scared. He wondered if anything could kill this figure if an arrow could not, but he drew his knife anyway. If an arrow could not do the job, perhaps a steel blade might.

"Are you an idiot, boy? The arrow made it plain that I am invulnerable." The knight made no move, but Faran felt a cold chill in his veins.

"I'm not an idiot. If an arrow can't shut you up, perhaps something else will."

Faran stepped closer, the knife high before him. "Was it you who destroyed Dromdruin?"

The knight watched him as a cat watches a mouse. Then he offered another of his strangely formal bows.

"I was given the honor of leading the men who did so."

Faran was beyond fear now. "Then I shall kill you."

The knight laughed, and the sound of it rang through the woods.

"I think not, boy. But I admire your courage. More than I do your wit."

The knight dismissed Faran then from his thoughts, and turned back to Nuatha.

"For all that we once shared, I am permitted to make you this offer. Leave now. Come no more to Faladir, and live. You cannot stop us now, and we have no wish to kill you. But we will if we must. Leave, and know peace. The *seventh* is a myth. There are only six of us…"

The words of the knight faded away, and his head tilted as if he considered some new thought.

"Unless … no, but it is not possible."

Nuatha took a step forward, and if he had looked an old man before, even if unnaturally calm given the circumstances, he appeared a warrior now.

"You seek to threaten me? You are as a child, no matter how your powers have grown. And you seek to offer me amnesty? Do not take me for a fool. You wish only for me to leave so that you can grow stronger still. So that you can plot your way forward. If I left Faladir, how long before your leader, for he is a king no more in my eyes, seeks to stretch forth his power beyond the borders of the ancient realm? How long? And how far? No. That will never come to pass! Not while I live, Lindercroft. And you know that in your heart. Or you would, if yours still beat with mortal spirit rather than the dark pulse of the Morleth Stone."

The knight seemed taken aback by the old man's words, but then he smiled. And he turned away from Nuatha, and Faran felt the weight of his cold gaze.

"It cannot be possible," the knight said softly, "and yet by your attempt to distract me, I sense it is true. At least, I sense that you believe it."

The shadowy figure, a thing of darkness but also silver bright, turned his gaze back and forth between the old man and Faran.

"You think this idiot is the *seventh*, Aranloth?"

8. I'll Kill You, Boy

The name just uttered shocked Faran. *Aranloth*. The greatest lòhren of them all. Old as the hills. Older. A wizard of immense power. A legend through all of Alithoras, and the founding of Faladir and the Kingshield Knights just one tale among a thousand.

And yet it made sense. The healer was more than he seemed. He carried the staff, even if his robes were brown rather than the white of a lòhren. He had a presence and a way about him that no vagabond healer could ever possess. Yet still, it rocked Faran to his core. He had no business with lòhrens and knights. None at all. He was only a hunter, if a good one. But the knight and his men had committed an unspeakable crime. That made it his business. And only a mere hunter or not, the knight *would* pay for that.

The knight turned to him again, and those eyes of his were like slivers of black ice that bored through what they saw like the wind of winter's heart cut through a man no matter how thick his coat. And just as mercilessly.

"Do you think *you* are the seventh, boy?"

Faran was not sure what that meant. But the cold anger that had grown in him since the destruction of Dromdruin flared to life.

"I'm a hunter. And that's what I'll be. You and your men ruined my home, and you killed everyone I ever knew. Good people that didn't deserve that. So I *will* be a hunter. I'll hunt you down, and I'll kill you."

Something of the cold anger that burned within him came through into his words, and it surprised even Faran how hard his voice sounded.

But the knight was not impressed. The sneer was on his face again, and he did not even bother to reply to Faran. Instead, he addressed the old man again.

"Are you a fool also? You cannot believe that boy is the seventh. He's so stupid that if he threw himself on the ground he'd miss."

Faran heard the contempt in those words, and he did not like it. His face flared red, and the gaze of Ferla upon him made it redder still. She said nothing, and he knew she did not believe him an idiot. But to be insulted like that stung him, and all the harder that she had heard it.

But anger was wasted emotion, and he knew it. He could not snuff it out though, but he could let that part of his mind that was above it, and clear, still think.

The arrow had been useless. Likely a knife would also, for this was a vision formed of mist and therefore there was nothing solid to strike. But the key then was that the figure *was* mist, no matter that it was shaped to look like a man. The knight was not really there at all.

He moved away out of the vision of the knight, and the knight ignored him in his smugness, continuing to speak to the old man.

Nuatha, or Aranloth as he was now revealed, answered the knight, and though he must have seen what Faran was doing, he ignored it.

"You either believe in the prophecy or not, Lindercroft. If you don't, why should you fear a village lad?"

"I fear nothing!" the knight shouted.

"But you do. I sense it so clearly. You are not yet so mighty as you say, and doubt gnaws at your heart. You have no reason to fear a hunter who has never learned the Way of the Sword, and yet you do. Why should that be?"

The knight stiffened, but when he replied his voice was normal again.

"I fear nothing under the sun, still less the ancient words of a senile old man. You have made your choices, and you will reap their rewards. The Kingshield Knights rise now above the destinies of mortal men. Prophecy? Nay. I do not believe. We are great now, and we are men who make our own destiny."

Faran had been listening, but he was acting on a plan also. If the knight was not really there, and made up of mist only, might that mist not be dispersed?

The arrow had certainly caused a ripple through the vision, but something larger than that would be needed.

Faran had found what he wanted. A branch lay on the ground, its leaves half gone, but it was twiggy and many dried leaves remained upon it. It would do.

The knight had ignored him, as though beneath his notice. He had called him stupid, but he had not said he lacked courage.

Faran summoned it now. He took a deep breath, and then in a smooth motion he bent down, picked up the branch and leaped at the knight.

The branch was not a weapon, as such. But he struck at the figure as though it was, thrashing it and waving it fast as he could through the misty image.

The knight wheeled upon him, and he drew the great blade that hung at his side. Faran had seen few swords before, but he had seen his grandfather's. This was like it. The hilt was jeweled and the blade pattern-welded, shimmering as it rose high.

But the mist dispersed. What sorcery held it together, Faran did not know. Nor did he care. Mist was mist. Wave something through it, and it moved and broke apart.

And this was what happened to the knight. His image faded away to mere glimmerings in the air, and last was his helmed head, the eyes dark pits of fury. But worse was the wispy voice of the knight, like the hiss of a snake fading away on a dying wind.

I'll kill you, boy.

It was disconcerting to hear, but nearly as bad was what Ferla said when the knight was gone, looking at him with large eyes.

"You're the seventh knight, Faran."

9. I Hate Them

Nuatha was the first to react, or Aranloth if that was who he truly was.

"You have courage, lad. Lindercroft is the type to hold grudges, and you humiliated him. That's what comes of calling someone stupid though, I suppose."

"Humiliation is the least that I'll do to him, if I ever meet him in the flesh."

The old man took a firm grip on his staff. "Maybe so, but never forget that he's a Kingshield Knight. He's a great warrior, and highly intelligent, and practiced in some forms of magic. Other forms … he's learning now. Face to face, he'd crush you. So keep that in mind, and hope that you don't meet him soon. You have a long way to go before you can think about fighting him."

Faran shook his head. "I'm not this *seventh*, that you keep talking about. And I don't want to be. I'll not fight him, but I'll put an arrow through him if I can."

"Well, that's as may be, but—"

Faran interrupted the old man. "Are you really Aranloth?"

The bright eyes of the healer studied him for several moments.

"I am."

"How is it possible for a man to live so long? Even a lòhren? And why didn't you ever tell us?"

"Magic has its uses, lad. It confers longevity. But that comes at a terrible price. And I have lived longer than even you guess, for the founding of Faladir, which is legend to you, is but a little while ago to me. Think on that, and what it means."

Faran stored that away to ponder, but he knew the lòhren had not answered his other question.

"But why lie? Why hide such a thing from us?"

The old man leaned on his staff again, and if the question disturbed him, he showed no sign of it.

"I have many names, Faran. In many places. I have as many, or more, enemies. It's not always wise for me to announce who I am. Not for me, or those I associate with. But your grandfather knew, of course. He was a knight after all. And he did not tell you either, so don't judge me too harshly."

It was a good point, and Faran knew it. But he still felt deceived.

"Why—"

It was the lòhren's turn to interrupt. "We have no time for this. Not now. If you haven't realized yet, the enemy knows where we are. We have to get out of here, and swiftly."

"I thought you said we shouldn't travel at night because of the elù-drak?"

The lòhren showed his first sign of impatience, and his eyes glittered.

"There are dangers, and then there are dangers. We are forced to do now what I would rather not, but life is like that. Better the elù-drak than Lindercroft and all his men. And there are other creatures that might be in service to him too. Now, are you ready to move, or will you wait for death to trample you down!"

The old man stalked away then, moving swiftly into the woods but quietly. Ferla followed after, and Faran, muttering to himself, took up their trail but hung back as far as he dared without losing them. But then he thought of the elù-drak, and quickened his pace.

They traveled down into a deep valley, and this was thicker with trees than Dromdruin, which made things dark as could be. Barely even a star could be seen glittering overhead.

They did not talk, which just now suited Faran. He had much to consider, and his mind shifted from topic to topic but found few answers.

For a while, he pondered what other creatures beside an elù-drak that the knight might control. His mind passed over the names of things that had fought in the Shadowed Wars, but it was disturbing to think that those things of legend might be real. He knew they must be, otherwise the tales that had come down from of old were lies. But it was one thing to hear rumor of them from stories and another to meet one face to face.

No. He would think no more on that. Especially in such a dark and grim place as the valley they now traveled. Bad enough that the elù-drak was real. He did not need to envision worse.

His thoughts turned to Aranloth next. Was the old healer really the lòhren of legend? He had admitted it. The knight had called him so. But it was still hard to believe. Yet, on reflection, no harder than the elù-drak. Both were legends. Both, he had now seen with his own eyes. And his grandfather had almost seemed to revere the man. That made more sense now.

His grandfather had been a proud man, friendly to all but distrusting. Yet he was close to the healer, and it all fitted together. The lòhren was the mentor of the knights. He *was* held in reverence by them, or at least so the stories said. And even Lindercroft had shown some of it, though it seemed they were now enemies.

That line of thought opened up new ideas to consider. Had the knights really fallen? The prophecy said they would, one day. Their sacred task was to guard the

Morleth Stone. But everyone knew they were destined to one day pick it up and use it. And the evil would taint them, and twist their spirits to the dark. Having met Lindercroft, it was not hard to believe.

But the stories had circulated for hundreds of years. Everyone knew the prophecy, but no one ever thought it would become reality in their own time. Yet it seemed that it had in his, and in its way that was more disturbing than an elù-drak or any other creature. The Morleth Stone was ultimate evil. It was ultimate power, too. If its power was waking, it would draw evil like moths to a flame. And if the king wielded it, the first among the knights, then the realm was in jeopardy and every soul living within it. Who knew what chaos would be unleashed, compared to which an elù-drak might seem as nothing?

They moved down to lower ground, in the heart of the valley. Faran had been further away from Dromdruin than this, but he had never been to this place. He had heard of it though.

He could not see much in the dark. But the trees gave way, and the ruins of an ancient city lay before them. Tall towers had tumbled. The city wall was a ruin of stones. The houses and buildings had collapsed. But not all. Here and there a house of stone endured, surviving against the odds.

The lòhren did not hesitate. He led them along what once must have been a main thoroughfare. He led them as though he knew the way, but whether because he had walked these streets when the city was alive, or learned their ways after its death, Faran did not know.

The city was older than Faladir though. Legend claimed it was an ancient ruin before Faladir was ever built.

Looking about him, Faran felt uneasy. They were in the open now, and his glance lifted often to the sky. Should the elù-drak return, they would be seen.

Yet Faran guessed why the old man led them this way. It was quick, for the streets ran straight and true, and it saved them a great deal of time that otherwise would have been spent finding a way through the thick woods. Time, that the lòhren must have believed precious.

It was yet another disturbing thought. It was one thing for Nuatha the vagabond healer to worry they might be pursued. It was another for Aranloth, the mightiest lòhren to ever walk the land, to fear it and take steps to escape.

They came to some sort of central square. No buildings were visible here, either as tumbled stones or still standing upright. But what once must have been a fountain stood in its center. This, Faran could just make out. It was a rearing horse, and water would once have tumbled from its wide mouth into the basin below.

Faran had never seen anything like it before. But his grandfather had told him of such things, and that many such fountains decorated squares and parks in Faladir.

They halted beneath it, using it as protection from the sky above while they rested for a short while.

"Where are we headed?" Faran asked the lòhren.

The old man's eyes gleamed in the dark. He was less Nuatha now, and more Aranloth.

"Anywhere will do at the moment, just so long as it's away from where we were. The farther the better. For that matter, the farther away from Faladir the better."

It was not what Faran wanted. Dromdruin had been his home, and he had been forced to leave. But all of Faladir was his home too. Must he leave everything behind?

But he knew the answer to that. As much as he wanted justice, as much as Lindercroft must pay for what he had done, he knew he was no match for the knight. He knew if he stayed, he would die.

"You've led us well," Faran said quietly. "More than that … you've kept us alive. I haven't been easy on you. But none of this has been easy."

Aranloth, for so Faran had begun to think of him, sighed in the dark.

"I know, lad."

"You were wrong about one thing, though."

The old main raised an eyebrow. "What was that?"

"You told the knight that I had not learned the Way of the Sword. That's not quite true."

Aranloth grinned in the dark. "Ah, I see. But know this, Faran. The art of warfare is to deceive the enemy. Learn that lesson well, for it will serve you all your life. If you want to go right, make the enemy think you're going left. If you wish to retreat, let them think you're attacking. If you're short of food, make them believe you have a surplus." The old man paused to brush away a mosquito that had landed on him. "And warfare takes many forms. Sometimes it's just words. When I said to Lindercroft that you didn't know the Way of the Sword, I was lying. I know your grandfather taught you the basics."

Faran was not really surprised. His grandfather would have mentioned something like that to the lòhren. The Way of the Sword was considered as being almost sacred. It was rare for a knight to teach it to someone not a knight, and possibly his grandfather had even asked permission of the lòhren.

"I was never very good at it though. Ferla is better with a sword than me, and she only learned off a farmer."

Aranloth shrugged. "I know that you weren't especially good. But you were young too. By the time you were old enough to really start learning, your grandfather was getting too ill to teach properly. He said you had talent, though. And he would have known. All the knights are great warriors, but he was one of the best with a sword that I ever saw."

Faran felt a surge of pride. He had not known *that*. But it brought the conversation around to another topic.

"I don't know what it is that you think, or for that matter what Lindercroft thinks, but I'm not the seventh knight. I know the prophecy, and I know it's not about me. I'm not up to that. And even if I were, I wouldn't do it."

Aranloth gazed back at him, and his face gave nothing away of what he thought.

"Did your grandfather ever tell you the secret of the Kingshield Knights?"

The question surprised Faran. He had expected the lòhren to be upset, or maybe even try to convince him otherwise.

"No, he never mentioned any secrets."

"Well, there is one. Your grandfather knew it. So did every other knight in a long line of them stretching back to the founding of the order."

"What is it, then?" Faran asked.

"Ah, but it's a secret. Only the knights know, and they don't tell."

"Then why bring it up?"

"Maybe because I'm a senile old man, as Lindercroft said. Or maybe I'm trying to get you to think on something. You decide."

"More riddles, Aranloth?"

"The world is full of riddles, but I think you'll discover the answer to this one soon enough."

Ferla stirred, and she ran a hand through her long hair. It was always a sign she was dissatisfied with something.

"Don't you *want* to be a knight, Faran? It's the highest honor in the land."

Faran felt old emotions bubble to the surface, but he kept his voice even and low.

"It *was* the highest honor. But you know what they did to my grandfather. They cast him out. The king stripped away his lands. He was rendered destitute, and died in poverty. It was the Kingshield Knights that did that to him, and not once, even as he grew frail and death approached, did one of them visit or send word. Not once did the king thank him for a lifetime of service. Do I want to be a knight? Never. I *hate* them."

His voice had crept up toward the end, and Faran closed his mouth with a click. He would *never* be a knight.

Aranloth stirred restlessly in the dark. "I do not blame you. I would never blame you for feeling as you do. What the king and the knights did to your grandfather was unforgivable. It was the beginning of the end for them, but this is true also."

Faran watched the old man closely. His voice had changed, and the glitter of his eyes was even brighter. There was something of the look about him that he had revealed in Dromdruin village. An inner strength shone out, and though he veiled his power, Faran began to sense how much more he was than an old man. He was not Nuatha the healer now, but Aranloth the lòhren, a terrible foe to his enemies and a bulwark against which evil had thrown itself for millennia, and retreated afterward in failure.

"A prophecy I made," he continued, "and my prophecies come true. A seventh knight will rise. I saw it in my mind long ago, born on the winds of magic as true prophecies are, and I voiced it. It *will* happen. But whether that seventh knight is you, or another, I cannot say. But that knight will rise, and this is the time."

A chill ran through Faran, but Aranloth was not quite done, even if his voice returned to normal.

"You are marked for death, lad. I'm not the only one with the power of foresight. The enemy learned something. They feared a threat from Dromdruin village, though I'll not say they think you're the seventh. But they destroyed the village, and you are from it and marked for death. It matters nothing whether you wish to be a knight or not. That is certain. The only matter for doubt is what do you intend to do about it?"

10. White Fire

The three travelers moved off again, for they had spent as much time as they dared resting. And it had been eerie too, beneath the fountain of a long-ruined city and contemplating the enemy who would see them destroyed.

Aranloth took the lead as usual, heading across the square. His robes glimmered palely, which was strange given that they were brown. But Faran kept his gaze upward for the most part, fearful of the elù-drak.

For her part, Ferla gazed upward too. She had said little, and he wondered what she thought about what was happening. He wanted to talk to her because he always found her view well-considered. But there would be no chance of that anytime soon.

The lòhren set a fast pace, and they followed quickly as he once again led them through ruined streets. But now, ever so slightly, the land began to slope downward. The old buildings were in worse repair too. Here, few remained upright, and those that had fallen were little more than mounds in the dark.

It was a dead city. But once a large number of people had lived here. They had worked and dreamed and feasted. They had gotten ill and better. They had lived and died and their children after them. But the only monument to their existence was tumbled ruins.

Faran was glad when they came to a long mound of rocks, which they clambered over.

"The city wall," Aranloth said to them quietly. "Or what's left of it."

Once they came down the other side, they were in the woods again, and Faran felt more comfortable.

Their pace slowed, as it must for all the obstacles. But that did not make it less tiring. They pushed ahead, and the lòhren found faint game trails to follow, which helped but did not solve their problem. There was no easy way to move through thick scrub, nor a quiet one either.

The ground continued to slope downward, but this was of little help. The lower ground was the cause of the thicker growth of trees and bushes, and it brought more and more mosquitoes. There must be a body of water nearby.

It did not take long to find it. To their left, bushes gave way to reeds, and the ground grew boggy. Aranloth veered a little to the right, and kept them from the worst of it, but now and then they heard the plonk of something entering water, and the frequent croaking of frogs.

The ground leveled after some while, and the noise of water receded, but the numbers of mosquitoes did not diminish.

Faran's mood grew dark. He preferred the ridges and the woods to swamps. And it irked him that somehow he had become a fugitive. It was yet one more crime, though the least of them, that he held against Lindercroft.

That made his thoughts even darker. He wanted to kill the knight, and he knew justice demanded it, for it seemed the king would offer none himself. If Dromdruin were to be avenged, it must be by him, but in truth, for all his words, he could not do it. He did not have the skill to fight a knight, and he was not sure that he could speed an arrow in the dark to take the man's life like an assassin.

That meant that maybe he would have to learn to fight. It was true that his grandfather had taught him something of the Way of the Sword. But he was not skilled. It would be a long and hard journey to even think about one day confronting a knight.

A mosquito buzzed by his ear, and he swatted away at it angrily. Even if he wished to learn how to fight, there was no one to teach him.

The thick brush opened up and they came to a clear area where a brook clattered over a causeway of shattered stones. No doubt it fed the bog lands, but at least here the ground was firm and on the other side they would probably begin to move upward again and leave the mosquitoes behind.

Aranloth went ahead, testing the water with his staff, but even out in the middle it remained little more than ankle deep.

The lòhren paused, as if in doubt, and then his head jerked upward as though seeking something in the sky. Even as he moved a terrible scream tore the night from above them.

Faran looked up, dreading what he would see. He had forgotten the terror of the elù-drak, but it overwhelmed him now, and it was worse than before. For now, beyond doubt, the creature had spotted them and it plummeted out of the darkness toward where they stood, revealed in the open.

The black wings were bent, and held rigid. It streaked through the sky, and now up close Faran saw it better. Bat winged it was, but the body was human. And it was female, it's naked skin pale against the blackness of its wings.

There was a face also. Beautiful but terrible. Long black hair streamed behind it. The wide-set eyes gleamed with a feral light. The red lips parted, and the scream came again.

Faran's knees went weak. But he drew an arrow from his quiver and loosed it.

His shot was wild. Ferla had loosed an arrow also, and hers hurtled past the creature much closer, but still missed.

The elù-drak screamed and swerved away, all dark wings and pale skin.

"Beware the spurs!" Aranloth cried. "They're poison!"

The old man led them quickly across the causeway, but they did not get far before the thing came again, swift as an arrow itself for all its size.

This time Faran saw the spurs on the elbow joints of the wing. They flashed wickedly, but he tore his eyes off the creature and together he and Ferla stumbled into a patch of trees. The air beat around them as the wings drew close, but turning and preparing to fight Faran saw that the thing had veered away again and now hurtled at Aranloth.

The lòhren stood tall, his staff held high and suddenly silver fire lanced from its tip and speared toward the elù-drak. It was the fabled lòhren-fire of legend, but the creature seemed to have anticipated it.

More agile than Faran could believe, the creature dropped low and dodged the deadly magic, but it still hurtled toward the old man.

But Aranloth was quicker than he looked also, and he leaped among the trees seeking to evade attack himself.

Faran and Ferla stumbled ahead. They sought more cover, but instead the trees gave way again and they were once more in a narrow glade.

White fire lanced through the dark once more, this time striking a tree and causing it to erupt in flame. Of the elù-drak, there was no sign, not by sight or by sound.

Faran stumbled but came up again quickly. Had Aranloth killed the creature? He did not think so. Had it been wounded, surely it would have cried out.

Too late he realized what had been done. Like a wolf hunting deer, the creature of the dark had separated its prey and now attacked the weakest.

There was a rush of wings from the side, and the elù-drak came straight at them.

Faran fumbled for his bow, but he would be too slow and he knew it. Then Ferla was there, crashing into the thing with her body and striking with her bow as a staff.

She saved him, but she paid a price, for the elù-drak screamed and landed in a tangled mess on the ground. But Ferla did not move after that, while the creature stood.

Bat winged she stood before him, naked and terrible. He glanced into her eyes, and then weakness flowed over him. It was all he could do to stand.

The dark wings furled behind her, and she moved toward him, a thing of terror and grace, pinning him with her eyes, and even when her red lips drew back to reveal glistening fangs in her mouth, he stood motionless, transfixed by her magic.

"Don't look into her eyes!" came the cry of the lòhren from behind him, but Faran knew it was too late for that, and he knew also that he stood between the creature and any attack the lòhren might make, but he could not back away.

The bow dropped uselessly from his hands. She leaped at him, drawing him into a dark embrace, and he felt the heat of her body against him and the hot breath of her mouth against his neck. Behind him, he heard the lòhren's scrambling approach, but the lòhren-fire, if the old man used it, would kill the both of them.

But even as she embraced him in a clasp of death, Faran felt some force within him flare to life. *He would not die like this.*

He smashed his head forward into her own, and her following scream pierced his ear. His unexpected move had hurt her. Perhaps she had not expected him to move at all, thinking her dark magic overpowering him, but the pain in his own head seemed to break her spell, and he drew a knife and stabbed her.

She screamed again, and reeled away. Faran stumbled after her, the bloody knife red in his hand. He must finish what he had begun, for if she did not die then he surely would.

But the lòhren was quicker than him. The old man jumped before him, and lòhren-fire lanced from his staff.

The elù-drak was not quick enough this time. The white-hot flame caught her even as she leaped upward to take flight.

A creature of deadly grace she had been, but now she tumbled to the ground, one leathery wing flaring with fire and hatred in her eyes.

She charged at Aranloth. Another burst of lòhren-fire struck her, and then something else flashed through the air. Ferla had crawled to her knees, and thrown a knife.

The blade caught the elù-drak in the chest, and red blood bloomed over her white skin. Then the lòhren-fire licked it, and the blood steamed away in a red vapor.

The creature screamed again, and her skin blackened while swathes of it peeled off. But she came again for the lòhren, teeth flashing.

Faran bent down and picked up his bow. Two arrows he sent into her body, and neither did the lòhren-fire relent. Yet still, screaming, she stumbled toward the old man.

The wings of the elù-drak were withered away by the heat, and a stench of burning flesh filled the air. Yet still she groped toward the old man, trying to get close enough to kill him.

Aranloth did not back off. He thrust his staff forth, and the lòhren-fire intensified. Like the sun, it was too bright to look at, and Faran turned away.

The elù-drak gave a final scream. She tumbled to the ground, and even in her death throes crawled toward the old man. But she died, for nothing could endure knife, arrow and fire for long.

The lòhren-fire winked out, and the clearing was engulfed in a great dark once more. He could not see her body. He could not see anything after that bright light, but he could smell her charred flesh, rank in the air.

There was silence. Faran's eyesight began to adjust to the dark once more, and he saw the lòhren move toward Ferla.

"Are you hurt?" he asked

She came unsteadily to her feet. "I don't feel very well," she answered. And she stretched out her arm for the lòhren to see.

Faran could not make anything out, but then a faint light started to glow at the tip of the old man's staff. And he saw the sleeve of Ferla's tunic was ripped, and a long, bloody groove along her arm.

"It was one of the spurs," she said quietly.

The old man held her arm gently, and studied the wound. Faran felt sick. The lòhren had warned them about the spurs, and even if he had not the legends told him what he needed to know. The spurs of the elù-drak were poisonous. And the poison was deadly.

Faran came closer. Ferla had saved him, for without her intervention he would have died before the lòhren could have reached him. He owed her his life. But the price of her gift might be her own life. He had never heard any story where the poison of an elù-drak did not kill.

He looked into her eyes, and she gave him a tight grin. But already he saw that something was not right with her, and that her face was deadly pale and her whole body was trembling.

Perhaps it was only fear and shock. But in his heart, he knew the truth. The poison was already spreading through her body.

11. Colder than Ice

Aranloth acted quickly.

"Give me a knife," he ordered, and Faran handed his over. The lòhren used it to cut away the sleeve of Ferla's tunic, and then he cut this into long strips and wrapped the material tightly around her arm, starting near her shoulder and working down.

"That will help," he said. But he was not done.

He pressed his palms against her arm, and muttered some words Faran did not catch. A white light glowed where he touched her, and the trembling subsided a little, but did not go away.

He withdrew his hands. "I've done all that I can, at least for the present."

"What do we do now?" Faran asked.

"Now, we need to get out of here. The elù-drak may not have been alone. And Ferla needs a fire and warmth."

"Have you cured her?" Faran asked.

The lòhren hesitated. "What I've done will hold the worst off for a little while. We need to move, and now. I know a cave close by. We can light a fire there, and we should remain hidden, for a while."

They made to move off, but Ferla stopped them.

"Wait," she said.

"We have to go," Faran answered. "We'll get you to somewhere safe."

She shook her head. "You didn't listen to Aranloth's answer just before. You asked if he had cured me, and his answer was that he had held the worst off, for a while." She straightened, and a look of determination steeled her face. "Aranloth knows, Faran. So do you if you think about it. Legend says the poison of an elù-drak is deadly."

Faran blinked away tears. "What are you saying?"

"I'm going to die, Faran. We all know it. Taking me with you will only slow you down. I won't have that on my conscience. I'll not allow you to be killed by your enemies. You must go without me."

Faran turned to the lòhren, but the old man gave no answer.

"I'm not leaving you behind. Now or ever. You're coming with us, even if I have to carry you all the way. You're all I have left of the village. I'm not leaving you as well."

"But what if I have to leave you? If it must happen, better here and now."

Faran had no answer to that, but it was the lòhren who intervened.

"No one is leaving anyone. Not if I can help it. You're not dead yet, and you may not die either."

Ferla turned to the lòhren. "But—"

"There's no time for buts. Now move! The two of you!"

And move they did. Faran put an arm around her to hold her steady, for she was weak in the legs, and they trailed after the old man who moved away with purpose.

They left the little clearing behind them, and the body of the elù-drak with it. Faran was glad of the dark, because he did not want to see what had become of her. But her screams haunted him, and he thought the smell of her burnt flesh would never leave him either.

The old man led them upward now, for they had come to the other side of the valley. The trees grew thickly again, although on this side there seemed to be many pines. They were hard to see, but the scent of resin filled the air and the soft crunch of deep layers of pine leaves softened the tread of their boots.

They hastened on, but it was not long before Ferla began to stumble. More and more Faran lent her his support, until at last he picked her up and carried her.

She placed her arms around his neck, but soon even the strength of her arms gave out and he carried her limp form in growing desperation.

She was not dead yet. He felt the slow rise and fall of her chest against his body, but her skin was cold and clammy.

Faran drove himself on. He would not let her down. He would not rest until they reached the cave Aranloth spoke of. She was all that he had left, and she had risked her life to save him. If she died, he would be responsible. Just as, in a way, he knew he was responsible for the death of all the villagers.

It did not matter if he was the seventh knight. He knew he was not, nor would he ever be. But for some reason the enemy thought he was. That was enough. He knew he was judging himself harshly, but he could not help it. Everyone had died for him, one way or another.

Guilt washed over him. But anger came with it. He wanted none of this. None at all. But circumstances had forced him into a situation from which there was no escape. Yet the one thing he had control over was what he did for Ferla. He was not a god to decide if she lived or died. But he would do anything possible to save her.

His legs began to cramp, but he walked on through the agony. His arms hurt, and his breath came in ragged rasps. Aranloth looked at him, and slowed their pace, but did not stop. Nor did Faran expect him to.

"Courage, Faran," the old man said to him. "We're close now."

They moved toward the top of the ridge, but the pines still grew thickly about them and there was no sign of a cave. Yet the lòhren slowed, and he wound in and out of the trees, climbing a steep slope.

Near its top he must have found what he sought, for he came to a stop.

Faran saw nothing, but after a moment the lòhren went ahead through a gap in the trees. The ground turned rocky, and just at its steepest there seemed to be a shadow darker than the other shadows.

"This is it," Aranloth said.

He led Faran inside. It was a narrow entrance, and Faran wondered how visible it would be even in daylight. But the old man had found it, and that was all that mattered.

The entrance widened quickly. A faint light shone once more from the tip of the lòhren's staff. The cave was much bigger than Faran would have thought, and he staggered to its center where he laid Ferla down gently. She was limp and unconscious. Quickly the old man bent down and felt the pulse at her neck.

"She yet lives," he said. But there was an element of surprise in his voice and fear stabbed into Faran's heart.

"What now?" Faran asked.

"We build a fire."

The old man moved toward the back of the cave, and there was a store of timber there. When the dim light of the staff allowed, he saw also that the ceiling was blackened by the smoke of many fires in the past. They were not the first travelers to use this cave.

They moved some of the timber closer to Ferla. Faran was worried that there was little in the way of tinder, and that the fire would be hard to start, but Aranloth surprised him.

"Stand back," the lòhren commanded.

Faran gave him room, and the old man lowered his staff. Lòhren-fire spurted from its tip, igniting the timber. It crackled and burned, and when the lòhren-fire vanished a few moments later, the flames faded away to a normal shade of orange.

The warmth of the fire was welcome, and Faran hoped it would help Ferla, but for himself his blood still ran cold with dread.

"Can you do something for her?"

The old man leaned on his staff, as he often did. He seemed poised and in command, yet there was a look in his eye that Faran could not interpret.

"The poison of the elù-drak is deadly, Faran. It works in two ways, and it attacks both body and spirit. For the body, I have already done what I can. And the fire will help. For the spirit…"

"I can't let her die, old man. I can't. There must be something you can do. Please."

The lòhren considered him a moment. "There's nothing I can do to aid her spirit. Such a thing, if it can be done at all, must be done by one who knows her well and that she trusts. For where her spirit wanders now is in a dark, dark place. It's driven there by the foul magic of the poison, and only one who knows her well can find her there, and only one she well trusts can guide her back."

"I'll do it," Faran said without hesitation.

The lòhren gazed at him with those eyes that saw everything, but they gave away nothing of what the lòhren himself was thinking.

"If you do it, you're risking your own life. More than risking it because the chances of you returning yourself are slim. Perhaps as slim as one in ten."

Faran looked down at Ferla where she lay, unconscious but trembling. Then he knelt and touched her cheek with the back of his hand. Her skin was colder than ice.

"I'll do it," he said. "I'll do whatever it takes, but it must be now. She has little time left."

12. You Are Your Own Man

The lòhren nodded slowly. "It will take all that you have, and perhaps more."

Faran did not doubt it. And he did not care. Guilt washed over him. People had died for him. Ferla had risked her life for him. He would do what it took, and to hell with the consequences.

"What do I do?"

"I will send you to join her in her spirit dream. Where you go will be a real place. What happens to you there will be real. If you are cut, you will bleed. If you are killed, you will die. It is a place like this world, but it is different. It is a realm of magic and mind also, much more than here. It is a—"

"Just send me there. I'll learn what I need to know when I'm there, or die."

The old man gave the slightest of shrugs. "Perhaps that's the best way. Doing is learning. Just remember, find Ferla and bring her back through the same place as you enter."

Faran gave a sharp nod. He was ready.

"Lie down beside her," the lòhren commanded.

Faran did so. He should have felt heat from her body, but she was cold as snow. Aranloth had not told him to, but he took her hand in his own. It was like limp ice.

The lòhren knelt down beside him, and placed the staff lengthwise across both of their bodies.

"Do not die there, Faran. Or this cave will be your tomb, and hers also. And come back the way you go in."

Faran nodded, but the lòhren had already begun to work his magic.

The old man muttered words, but his voice was so soft that Faran could not hear them properly. They might have been Halathrin, the language of the elves, although Faran was not sure. But whatever words he spoke, they were words of power. The cave grew dim. Light and life seemed to recede into the distance. He tried to keep his eyes open, but a great weariness overpowered him and forced them closed.

The weight of the staff across his chest became more noticeable. Then swiftly it grew until it felt like a log had fallen across his body. It was a crushing weight. It was like a mountain upon his chest and panic surged through him.

"Be at peace," the voice of the lòhren whispered through his mind. "Come back the way you go in. There is no other way to return. You go to a place of spirit rather than flesh. Your mind is both armor and weapon. Remember."

The weight was suddenly gone. The cave was gone, and the fire and the scent of smoke also. There was only a great dark, and Faran drifted through it.

He may have drifted while ages of the world turned and the stars shifted course in the sky, or he may have drifted but the time it takes to wake from sleep. He was not sure which, for it seemed both at once, but wake he did.

And it was not dark. Nor was it the cave. He was by a river, and its water was black, and across it spanned a bridge to the other side. Down, far below, the black water rushed and seethed among shattered rocks and broken boulders.

Fear gripped him. It was light, but a murky light as though bushfires had besmirched the sky with clouds and hidden the sun behind a ruddy veil. He saw no sign of it, nor did he feel its warmth. But it was not cold either. He was in a nowhere place, but that place was close to another. It was on the verge of death. Final, ultimate, implacable death. Panic rose within him, and nearly he turned back, but he knew that if he did so Ferla would die.

He steeled himself, and took a few steps toward the bridge. It was a rickety construction of frayed rope and weathered timber slats. It would not bear his weight, and to try to walk upon it was to risk falling to the jagged stones far, far below.

If you are killed, you will die. Aranloth's warning rang like a bell through his mind. This was like a dream, but it was real.

He summoned his courage and put a foot upon the bridge. It moved at his touch, swaying precariously. But he did not step back. He could not. Better to die than to return in failure. Better to die than to leave the only friend he had to face death by herself.

He placed his other foot upon the bridge. Fear stabbed at him. The rocks below seemed to leer at him, so he fixed his gaze at the other end of the bridge and looked there only. He could see little, for the air in this place was hazy as though with smoke, but he detected no scent of it.

He moved across the bridge, slow step after slow step. The more the fear attacked him, the more he ignored it. This was nothing. This was walking one pace at a time. The bridge would hold his weight. Or it would not. It mattered nothing to him, either way.

So he told himself, and the more he repeated those thoughts to himself, the more he believed them.

The bridge did not give way. He touched the earth on the other side, and relief flooded through him. But he ignored that, too. This was no time nor place to let emotion control him. Instead, he must control his thoughts and actions as a potter shaped a clay vessel to his touch upon the wheel.

He moved forward. The earth was parched to dust, and this moved at his passage but fell back down again swiftly when he was gone. There was no breeze. There was no sun. There was no life here, and yet the sense of unseen gazes upon him flared to life.

Someone was here. Or something. But he was not interested in that. He had thoughts only for Ferla. How was he to find her? The lòhren had not said.

But just thinking of her, he sensed her presence. There was a road, flat and dusty and lifeless. She was farther along it, though how far he could not say. But he knew it with certainty. And if there were eyes gazing at him, and danger for him, then it must be so for her also.

He quickened his pace. The bridge, he realized now, had been a test of courage. Though who had set it, or why, he did not know. Perhaps this place drew his own fears and thoughts from his mind, and made them reality. He did not know, but he knew he had learned a life lesson crossing it. Fear had to be faced. In courage, there was strength. In despair, only failure. A person had to do what they must. And what they must do, they could endure.

He moved ahead through the dusty silence. But the sense of being watched was loud in his thoughts. It was a strange way to think of it, but his perceptions here were different. Still, he would trust them. He trusted nothing else.

Swiftly, but still carefully, he moved along, following the trail of Ferla through the link he felt to her. Whether it was the lòhren's magic, or his own connection to her as the lòhren had said, did not matter.

It did not surprise him though when three figures emerged from their hiding place among a patch of stunted trees. These were responsible for the sense of unseen gazes that he had felt upon him, only now they no longer wished to remain invisible.

They spread out as they approached him, and he knew what that meant. They were tall figures, and moved lithely. They had the look about them of warriors, only they were not men.

As men they walked, but their eyes burned with a red light. Horns grew from their heads, twisted and curved. And fangs protruded from their snout-like mouths.

Faran did not stop walking. He moved toward them, and this he saw they did not expect. A moment they paused, and then they came on to meet him.

As one they drew blades. These were of silvered steel, and the hilts were made of bone. They advanced, their eyes hungering for bloodshed, and Faran forced himself forward.

There was nowhere else for him to go. If he ran, they would pursue him. If he tried to go around them, they would block him. Nothing would take him toward Ferla except the direction he now headed.

And yet he was heading toward death. These things, whatever they were, carried swords. He had nothing save his hunting knife, and it would not serve against enemies such as these.

He wished for his bow. With that, he could protect himself. With that, he could kill them all. But it was not with him.

He drew his knife. It was small in his hand, but the blade glittered brightly. It felt strange though, almost weightless as if it was not really there.

It was a stray thought, and he needed to concentrate on the three figures. They were close now, but the feel of the knife in his hand disturbed him. It could *not* weigh less than it did in the real world.

And yet it did. Why should that be? Unless, perhaps, it was not a thing of the real world but a thing of his mind in this otherworldly place. And for that matter, why did he have the knife but not his bow and arrows? This was a place of spirit, the lòhren had told him. *Your mind is both armor and weapon.*

The three figures were close now, and they circled him. Soon, the killing would begin.

They did not talk, these men who were not men. But their every move spoke of death. Faran watched them, and fear surged through him. But with it came anger.

He wished for his bow, and then it occurred to him that perhaps he could make one from his thought. He pictured his yew bow in his hand, strung and knocked with an arrow. He pictured the honey-colored timber of the limbs, the straight shaft of ash for the arrow, tipped with steel and flighted with goose feathers.

He pictured it, and it filled his hands. And he did not hesitate to use it. Swift as thought he loosed the arrow and it buried itself in the chest of the creature before him.

Faran did not draw an arrow from a quiver. Instead, he pictured another arrow already strung, then drew and shot it at the attacker to his left. This figure staggered as the shaft tore away his throat, and then collapsed to the ground.

Faran was already turning to face the third, but he was too slow. He could not draw in time, and instead used the bow as a staff to block the sweeping blade that would have killed him.

Even so, the silvered sword shattered the timber and struck him a glancing blow on the shoulder. He felt the slow drip of blood there even as he reeled away.

Faran drew his knife. At a thought, the blade lengthened and it became a sword. The creature leaped at him, screaming, even as Faran raised his bright blade high.

Sword crashed against sword. A screech of metal tortured the air, and sparks flew.

Faran backed away. It had been only one blow, one meeting of blades, but he knew he was outmatched. The horn-headed man was the better fighter. And he came in at him, pressing hard to ensure that there was no room to use a bow again.

Faran reeled back, blocking strikes more by luck than by skill, but as suddenly as the attack started, it ceased. The horn-headed man fell to his knees, blood dripping from his mouth. Faran could not understand what had happened.

But then he saw a man behind the attacker, and that man's sword dripped blood. Somehow, a rescuer had come to his aid. How, and for what purpose, Faran could not understand. He had thought he would be alone here.

The new figure, a tall man in chainmail, his bright sword held casually before him, spoke.

"You did well, lad. Few are so quick to grasp how things work here." He pointed with his sword at the bodies that lay around them. "They took you for easy prey. But they were wrong."

Faran looked at the bodies. Even as he did so their flesh melted away and dispersed in a black, greasy smoke. All that was left was a humanlike skull, dazzling white and topped by those strange horns.

"Who *were* they?" he asked.

The newcomer shrugged. He drew a cloth from his tunic and cleaned his blade. "Perhaps they were once men. Or beasts. Maybe they were demons. But whoever they were, they'll not trouble you again. But that does not mean you're safe. There are other things that dwell in this foul shadow land."

Faran looked at his rescuer. There was something familiar about him, but he could not place it. And the silver helm on his head covered most of his face.

"Who are you? Why did you help me?"

"I'm not sure that you needed help. You seemed to be doing well without me."

"No, that last one would have killed me."

"Perhaps. But now we'll never know. And believe me, it's better that way."

"You still haven't told me who you are."

"That's because I'm not permitted to. But maybe you'll guess before you go back."

"I can't go back. I have to find Ferla. She needs me."

"Ah yes, the girl. I heard rumor of her. She did well also. At least, she's still alive in this place. Which is saying the same thing."

"I have to find her," Faran said. "And take her back home."

The other man nodded. "Do you mind if I come along?"

Faran was instantly suspicious. "Why?"

"Had I wished to attack you, lad, I'd already have done so. You have no reason to fear me, and I offer you help. Help that you may need."

What he said was true, but this was not the sort of place where anyone offered help.

"Why would you do that, though?"

"Perhaps I'm just bored. Or maybe I have a reason. You'll know if you discover who I am."

The man *did* seem familiar, but Faran just could not place him. He had known no warriors except his grandfather, and this was a much younger man, in the prime of his youth.

Faran gave a slight bow. "Thank you for helping me just now, and, if you wish, you're welcome to come with me. The truth is, I need all the help I can get."

The other man offered his own bow, far more polished, as though he had been at court.

"This is a land," he said, "where we tend to get what we fear, but also what we want. I'll be pleased to accompany you, but let us move swiftly now. Your friend is in danger, and it's never wise to spend too much time in the one place. Not in this shadow realm."

They moved ahead, but they did not talk. The warrior seemed comfortable with this, and seemed quite at ease. But his gaze moved around continuously, always searching for enemies. At times, he even stopped and studied their backtrail.

Faran was impatient, but he said nothing. He could not help Ferla if he died, and the warrior was helping to keep him alive. Several times there was movement far away from the road, but whoever or whatever it was receded back swiftly into cover and left them alone.

Faran would certainly leave the warrior alone. He was an imposing figure, and his every movement spoke of deadly grace. He was not someone to attack lightly.

The road began to climb. The dust turned to loose rocks that crunched beneath their boots, and they moved now into a series of low hills. The land watched them here, and Faran felt its malevolence.

The warrior glanced at him, as if he read his thoughts. And maybe he could.

"This is an evil land. Nothing lives here, except the land itself. It senses us, and our purpose. But do not fear. A spirit of courage and hope can survive it."

"How can the land be alive?"

What answer the warrior would have given, Faran did not learn. The man drew his sword, and the bright blade glimmered.

There must be enemies somewhere, but Faran saw nothing until the knight raised his sword to the horizon and pointed into the air. Then he saw what approached.

It was a flock of birds. Black they were, and they flew swift and straight as an arrow toward them. There were perhaps twenty, and a strange croaking sound drifted dimly to Faran's ears.

"Hrolgar," the warrior said, and he spoke with distaste. "They are the carrion birds of this place, though often they'll not wait for something to die before they eat it. They are harmless enough by themselves, but a flock is dangerous."

Faran watched them approach. "Then let's see how they deal with arrows."

Once more he pictured his bow, and it appeared in his hand. He did not marvel at that. It was simply the way of this place, so he accepted it.

He drew and loosed the arrow in one motion. It hissed through the air, but the Hrolgar separated and allowed the arrow to fly through where they had been. Then they drew close together again, and came on.

"Be careful of your eyes, Faran," the warrior warned. "They'll seek to blind you first."

Faran watched them come on. He had no liking for carrion birds, though they served their purpose in the wild. But he felt the malevolence of these, and he did not like it.

The arrow had been useless. What he needed was many at once. But no such thing was possible.

Yet neither was just summoning a bow by thought. So thinking, he tried a new tactic. He imagined another arrow notched to the string, and then drew and shot. He aimed for the middle of the flock, but before the arrow reached them, and even as they separated once more, he imagined the arrow separating in its flight to become ten different shafts.

Even as he thought it, so it occurred. The flock of Hrolgar wheeled and turned in flight, but swift as they were still four of them were hit by shafts and plummeted to the ground.

The two travelers in this strange land watched as the Hrolgar banked and beat their wings rapidly to move away.

"You learn fast indeed, lad."

Faran was uncomfortable with the compliment. "The faster I learn, the quicker I can reach Ferla."

The warrior looked around once more, assessing both sky and land for enemies.

"Then let us proceed. We're close now, for this is not a large land, and she has not been here long."

They moved ahead, and Faran wondered how his companion knew so much about this place. And, not for the first time, he wondered as well who he was and why he always kept his face hidden with the helm.

Soon, they descended into a valley. It was darker here, and there was a tang of smoke in the air. They shuffled down the slope, raising a trail of dust behind them, but it settled quickly as though movement or change was not welcome in this place.

They reached the bottom, and for the first time there were proper trees. At least, there were many of them and they reached a good height, but it was like no forest Faran had seen before.

The trunks of the trees were crusted with lichen and putrid-smelling fungus. Many had fallen, and lay rotting on the ground. But it seemed to Faran that those still standing were nearly as badly rotted. They looked like they might topple at any moment.

But he did not care. The warrior had been right, and he sensed that Ferla was close now. Whatever link joined them, it throbbed in his mind, and he turned a little to the left.

"This way," he said.

The warrior followed him deeper into the trees. Whether it was just a place to be cautious, or whether the other man had sensed some greater danger, he had drawn his sword.

Whatever the case, Faran sensed Ferla close by, and he paused. Then swiftly he ran to his left, leaping through the trees and entering a clearing. Ferla was there. But she was surrounded by a group of hideous creatures.

They came at her from all directions. Some slithered on pale bellies. Some trod the dusty ground with cloven hooves. Some flitted in the air, waiting to dart in and attack.

She held them all at bay with a sword in one hand and a shield in the other. But there was desperation written on her face, and Faran leaped into the fray, barely pausing to summon a sword into his hand that burned with a cold blue light.

He drove into the foul creatures, meting out death, and the warrior came with him. Ferla also seemed renewed with hope, and she danced through the fray with her sharp-edged sword.

It was too much for her attackers. They scattered and fled with hisses, yelps and growls. Faran and Ferla looked at each other, and something passed between them unspoken. Perhaps it was the recognition of trust.

"I had a feeling you would come for me, Faran."
"Always."

Her gaze shifted to the warrior, and there was less trust there, but she knew also that he had fought with Faran.

"Who's he?"

The warrior answered before Faran could. "A friend, for a little while. In a place where friends are few. And a guide also."

Faran gave a slight nod to Ferla. "He has been both those things."

"I would do more," the warrior said. "But that is all I am permitted here. Still, I can tell you this. Do not tarry. There is always danger, and the longer you are away from your bodies the harder it is to return. Go swiftly, now. Hasten."

"And when I return to my body, will I survive the elùdrak poison?"

The warrior gazed at her solemnly. "If the poison was too much for your body, you will not be able to return. But Aranloth would not have sent you help unless there was some hope. Whether that is enough, you will not know until you have reached the border of this land."

They ascended the slope of the valley then, and the warrior came with them. Faran wondered how he had known of Aranloth. He had not told him that. More and more he tried to piece together who this man was.

At the rim of the valley, Hrolgar waited. It was a larger flock this time, though whether it comprised some of the same that had attacked earlier, or were different ones, Faran did not know. But they kept a watchful distance, perched in stunted trees and croaking to themselves disconsolately.

The travelers hurried back along the road, but of their passage here earlier there was no sign. No tracks marked the dusty road, yet the skulls of the horned men remained, though now they seemed ancient things, bleached by long years of weathering.

They came at length to the deep ravine. The river ran through its course far below, the black water silent and the sharp rocks menacing. The bridge seemed even more rickety than it had before.

"This is where we part, Faran," the warrior said.

"It must be so," Faran answered. "Yet I wish otherwise. But the dead cannot cross to the lands of the living."

The warrior tilted his head slightly, and the silver helm gleamed.

"You know who I am, then?"

"I should have known from the beginning. But I know now. You're my grandfather."

The warrior removed his helm. It was not his grandfather, at least as he had known him. It was his grandfather in the prime of his youth, tall and strong and with a light in his eyes that Faran had not seen in his old age, after all that he loved had turned upon him.

His grandfather held out his hand, and Faran took it in the warrior's grip.

"I miss you," Faran said.

"And I you," his grandfather answered. "But I'm proud of you, and what you have become."

Faran was not sure what was meant by that. "Aranloth did not want me to do this," he said. "He wants me to be the seventh knight, and he did not want me to risk my life coming here. But I'm glad I did."

His grandfather sighed. "You are your own man, as hunter or knight or whatever you may be. The choice will be yours. But you are wrong about Aranloth, lad."

"Do you think so?"

"I know him better. Trust him. He sent you here, did he not? But had you not asked to come, especially thinking he did not wish it, he would have known at that moment that you could never be a knight. A knight must be the best of men."

His grandfather placed the helm on his head again, and even as he did so he began to fade. Like mist on the wind he disappeared.

"I miss you, grandfather!"

A voice came back in reply, distant like the memory of summer in winter's heart.

"We will meet again. Until then, be your own man. Always."

Then his grandfather was gone, and Faran realized Ferla had reached out to hold his hand.

Faran turned. It was time to go back to the real world, for he wished to be in this place no longer.

"There's the bridge," he said, pointing.

But Ferla shook her head. "I see no bridge, though this is where I crossed. All I see now though is the steep ravine."

Faran could not understand. The bridge was plain to see, if more rickety than it was entering this land.

"But it's just there…"

His voice trailed away as he saw the look on her face.

"It's too late for me, and I've been in this place too long. The way back is closed, and I'm dead."

A moment Faran stood there, at a loss. Then he straightened.

"Close your eyes," he said. "Trust me, for I can see the way."

He had a sudden feeling that time was running out. He had intended to lead her across the bridge, but now he scooped her up into his arms and carried her to the start of the bridge.

Her soft breath feathered his neck, but he knew that the thread of her life was drawn tight. Without pause, he stepped onto the timber slats, and the bridge swayed and trembled.

He would die here, or he would live. The bridge would hold his and Ferla's weight, or it would not. Hesitating, waiting, or going slowly would not change that. But if time was as short as he thought, then Ferla would die if he did not cross swiftly.

With a silent wish to the universe that all would be well, he darted nimbly over the bridge. It swayed and tilted, and a sudden roar of the black water came up to him from far below.

Halfway over, Ferla became a weight on his arms that he could barely lift. It was as though this shadow land was trying to draw her back. He was not nimble now. Each step was like walking in deep water.

Somehow, he made it to the other side, and there he cried out in pain for the cramps in his arms and legs, and he fell.

Darkness swallowed him, and the world turned and swam.

13. The Illusion of Reality

The stars wheeled in the void, and Faran felt the vastness of the great dark. All of time was but a single moment, each breath a thousand eternities.

Spinning and thrashing, he burst once more into the light. Aranloth's staff tumbled from across his body, and he looked over at Ferla. There was color to her skin again, and when he touched her cheek he felt warmth. The poison of the elù-drak had run its course, but had not killed her. He had not let it, and he felt tears well up in relief.

But there was no one to see, for which he was glad. Ferla still slept, and of Aranloth there was no sign. Where was he? Surely he would not have left them at such a time.

But then he heard voices outside, from somewhere near the cave entrance. Tired as he felt, weak and trembling from the experience that he had endured, he picked up his bow, gathered Aranloth's staff, and made his way carefully to the opening.

There, in the gray light of dawn, Aranloth stood his ground against at least a dozen soldiers. He stood in the cave entrance and barred the way, though it was clear that fear of him being a lòhren would not prevent the men acting sooner or later. The threat of violence charged the air.

Even with his bow, and swift as he was at using it, there were too many for him to kill. He would hit at best two, perhaps three, before they were upon him. And the lòhren was a legend, yet he could not face as many men as this and still prevail. At least, Faran did not think so.

Quietly, he moved beside the old man and slipped the staff into his hand. Those blue eyes gazed deep into his own. There was no fear there. There seemed no worry. But perhaps there was a hint of relief. He had returned, something the lòhren must have doubted. Having been to that strange shadow land, Faran understood why.

"Put down the bow, boy," one of the soldiers said. "You might hurt yourself."

Some of the other soldiers snickered, but Faran felt his anger rise. He was tired of being called boy. He was a man, and he was capable of a man's deeds.

Swift as thought, he drew an arrow from his quiver and nocked it.

"The next tin-headed soldier that calls me boy will get an arrow through his eye. So go ahead, and say it. If you dare."

They did not like that. They did not like it at all, and they eyed him with greater wariness. But they did not call him boy again, and even Aranloth raised an eyebrow at his tone. Not in rebuke, for the situation called for it. It was likely surprise.

"You can't kill more than one of us with that bow," the lead soldier said.

"At *least* one," Faran replied. "And that'll be the first man who moves."

They did not answer that. But their leader, an older man, for all that he was wary did not show signs of true fear. Anxiety, perhaps. But not fear. And no doubt he was weighing up the consequences of backing down. He must answer to Lindercroft, and that knight did not strike Faran as one who well tolerated the failure of those he led.

The tension grew. The air was thick with it. Furtively, the soldiers glanced at one another, but most often at their leader.

Faran sensed they were building up to an attack. But at least Lindercroft was not there, nor his other men. Just maybe, there would be a way to survive this.

But even as the air became charged with impending violence, a new figure strode across the slope toward them. That figure drew all eyes, and well it might.

The figure was clad in black, cowled and cloaked, and in its hand was a wych-wood staff.

Faran stifled a groan. He had feared Lindercroft or more men, but this was worse. Aranloth had said that dark things stirred, and this must surely be an elùgroth, a sorcerer of the dark. What pit of doom had spawned this dark day? But he gritted his teeth and took a firmer grip on his bow. The elùgroth was the greatest danger. He would be the first target of any arrow.

The black figure strode closer, all arrogance and power. Faran risked a glance at Aranloth, and the old man gazed at this newcomer with sharp intensity.

The elùgroth drew to a stop before them. And Faran saw that he was wrong. It was not a man, but a woman. Beneath the cowl she wore a haughty expression, and her eyes glittered. Her face was beautiful, but there was a hardness to it. Even the old man let out a long breath that he had been holding.

The woman pulled back her cowl, and Faran saw her face clearly now. He had not known that evil could be so beautiful. She took his breath away. She was young, but her eyes were old. They were green flecked with brown, or brown flecked with green. He could not decide which. But either way, they were hard as stones. Harder even than he had at first thought. And her hair was somewhat like her eyes. Not in color, but in that it too seemed a blend of two different things. It was blonde, but an ash blonde.

She gave the old man a dismissive glance. Then she turned to the soldiers.

"Fools!" she said. Her voice was not loud, and yet when she spoke it was with such authority that even an insult seemed a command. The soldiers drew close to one another, but they did not meet her gaze.

"Fools," she muttered again, almost to herself this time. "The Great Knight will not be happy with you. Why do you waste time and let fall the charge given to you?"

The lead soldier seemed confused. He was older, and more experienced than those he led, yet still this was too much for him. Faran did not blame him. He was at a loss himself.

The older soldier offered a bow. "How so? We have them. These are the ones we have been pursuing, and Lindercroft will reward us well. We've captured them."

Of all the reactions that Faran had expected from the sorceress, mirth was not one of them. Yet she threw back her head and a silvery laughter burst forth.

But as swift as it came, her mood changed again. "Idiot. Must the Shadow always work with the inept and incompetent? You have nothing! Can you not discern illusion from reality?"

With a sudden motion she stabbed at Aranloth with the tip of her staff.

Faran lifted higher his bow and nearly loosed the arrow he had nocked, but then slowly he lowered it again. The staff had passed straight through the lòhren. His figure became misty, but when she withdrew it he solidified again. But how that was possible, he did not know.

Aranloth spoke now, his voice taunting and a mischievous grin on his face.

"You'll not catch us now."

The sorceress leaned on her staff, and she looked directly at the lead soldier. Perhaps he was a captain. Faran did not know such things. It seemed to him just now that he knew nothing, for nothing made sense.

"Your quarry has escaped you," she said after a moment. "And while you dally with the illusion Aranloth left, your enemy escapes."

"It cannot be so," the lead soldier said, but there was doubt in his voice and anguish in his eyes.

"Verily, it is so," the sorceress answered. "Those you pursue have backtracked. That Aranloth is a wily fox, but I know his tricks. Follow me, and you may yet redeem yourself. Perhaps."

The lead soldier spat. He was not happy. In near disbelief, Faran watched as he led his men away and followed fast after the elùgroth.

When they were well out of earshot, Faran found his voice.

"What just happened?"

14. The Best Sort of Illusion

The old man grinned, and he seemed much younger. Merriment danced in his eyes.

"What just happened? A stroke of luck," he answered. "And surely, we were due for some. That was no elùgroth, but a lòhren."

Faran shook his head. "But the black clothes, and the wych-wood staff? How do you know she was a lòhren instead of what she seemed?"

Aranloth laughed. "I know each and every lòhren that ever was. And I know her. I know her well. We've had not just a stroke of luck, but very great luck."

The old man grew suddenly serious once more. "Yes indeed, we've been lucky. But it's our job to make the most of it now."

Faran still did not understand. "But her staff … it just went straight through you like the illusion she said you were. Are you really here?"

The old man laughed again. "It was illusion, alright. And the best sort. Illusions, like lies, are better believed the closer to the truth they are. And in this case, it was both a lie and an illusion. For I am real," and the old man gripped Faran's shoulder while he spoke to prove it, "but the staff was illusion. At least, it's appearance and length. She did not poke me with it. Nor would you have felt a thing had she poked you. But that was not needed, for the soldiers believed her falsehood. They knew there was illusion, for they saw it. But they followed her lead and accepted that it was me and not the staff."

There were footsteps behind them. They turned, and Ferla approached.

"What's been happening?"

Faran felt a surge of joy at seeing her standing up and walking. A look passed between them, and he knew she remembered what had happened in that shadow world.

"There's no time to explain now. The enemy nearly had us, but we were saved from fighting. Faran can tell you the rest while we walk. Are you feeling well enough for that?"

"I feel tired. Tired as though I've been sleeping for a week but somehow never managing to get proper rest. But I'll be alright. I can walk."

They left a few moments later. The lòhren led them, all traces of his humor gone. Faran guessed that he had been surprised, and he guessed also that such a thing did not happen to the old man often.

They did not travel swiftly, for Aranloth led them farther uphill and through the thickest and roughest terrain he could find. But he kept an eye on Ferla, and he did not push her beyond her limits. But she was strong, and even as she walked she seemed to gather strength instead of lose it. The poison of the elù-drak was but a memory.

After some hours they crested a hill. It was not open land, and there was little view in any direction, but it was high, and even amid the thick growth of trees there was still a cooling breeze.

Aranloth called a halt. He leaned on his staff, casual but carefully looking Ferla over for any ill effects of the morning's effort. Apparently, he was pleased with what he saw.

"You two stay here," he said. "You've earned a rest. But I think I'll do a bit of scouting and see what there is to see."

He walked away then, merging into the forest as well as any hunter ever could.

"Does that old man ever rest?" Ferla asked.

Faran had often wondered the same thing. "I don't know. He must, but perhaps he uses magic to sustain himself. What about you though?"

She stifled a yawn. "I'm tired. I think I'll just close my eyes for a bit."

She laid herself down, and after a moment Faran did the same. He felt it too. He had slept in the cave, but it was not true sleep. That other world may not have been real, not in the truest sense, but it had drained him. It must have been worse for Ferla.

He closed his eyes as well, thinking to just rest for a little while, but instead he fell into a deep and dreamless sleep.

When he woke, he knew instantly that hours had passed. He looked about fearfully, ashamed that he had been so careless, but there was no sign of any enemy.

Ferla was sitting up close by, and she was looking at him with an intense gaze. The lòhren had returned, but he stood higher up on the crest of the hill, perhaps looking for any sign of pursuit even through the thick growth of trees.

"Aranloth told me what you did for me," Ferla said.

Faran shrugged. "We were both there in that other place. You know I didn't really do much."

She shook her head. "You did enough, once there. But that's not what I meant."

"What did you mean then?"

"I meant how you came to be there in the first place."

"Aranloth sent me, that's all. With magic."

"Lòhrengai," she corrected him. "That's what it's called in the old tales."

"Lòhrengai, then. He sent me. I couldn't have done it otherwise."

"That's *still* not the point."

He frowned. "What *is* the point then."

"The point is that you volunteered to come. He said that he couldn't do it, but that you could. He said you were likely to die. And you came anyway. Thank you."

Faran shrugged. "You would have done the same for me?"

"Would I?"

That shocked him. "Wouldn't you have?"

"Of course I would have! But that's not what we're talking about."

Faran did not understand any of this. But so much had happened lately that he did not understand that he was getting used to the feeling.

"What *are* we talking about then?"

She looked away into the forest, but her reply was still intense.

"Tell me why. That's what I want to know. *Why?*"

This time, Faran looked away. He had always thought of Ferla as an older sister. She was someone he looked up to. Someone he admired. And because they were both hunters and loved the wild lands, they shared a connection.

But was it more than that? Sometimes it was. He had feelings for her. The older he had grown, the stronger those feelings became. When she lay dying, those feelings rose up stronger than ever. He could not bear to lose her. Yet he knew she felt none of this for him. To her, he had always been, and would always be, like a younger brother.

He did not look at her when he answered. "I don't know. You needed help, so I just did it. I'd have done the same for Aranloth."

He knew straight away that he had said something wrong. Her eyes hardened, but it was the old man who saved him from whatever she was about to say. She had a sharp tongue when she wanted to be cutting, and he saw that telltale narrowing of her eyes that signaled something like that was coming.

Aranloth strode down the slope. "It's time to go."

"Have you seen the enemy?" Faran asked.

"No. We're safe for the moment. Kareste has seen to that. But we need somewhere to hide and rest properly. And some way to throw the enemy off our trail."

They set out once more, and Faran thought of this Kareste person. She must have been Aranloth's lòhren friend. She had risked herself to lure the enemy away, and from Aranloth's words it was clear that at some point her ruse must unravel. He could not help but wonder what would happen to her then?

15. I Serve No Kingshield Knight

Kareste led the band forward, and she set a punishing pace. That way it was harder for them to ask any questions. Questions, just now, were her enemy.

She did not know enough of what was happening to answer anything properly. Elù-drak she had seen, and Lindercroft as well. Him she knew, but it had surprised her to see an elù-drak report to him. It should not have, for Aranloth had sent word that the knights had fallen, but it was still a blow.

So she walked swiftly, drew haughtiness around her like a cloak to help shield her from conversation with the captain, and listened intently to every scrap of talk among the men. From them, she could hope to piece together the other things she needed to know to keep them following her long enough for Aranloth to escape.

She owed the old man a lot. She owed him everything, including her status as a lòhren. For him, she would do anything, and risk anything.

And so she had, for this band of soldiers would try to kill her if she could not dissemble long enough to find a way to escape. But she did have a plan for that.

The sense of mistrust grew behind her. She felt it, and all the more so as they grew increasingly quiet. The captain broke that silence, nearly running to catch up to her, and he did not like it. He was a man used to exercising authority, and here it had been taken from him.

"Where are we headed?" he asked.

It might have been a question. But the tone of his voice was one of command. He expected an answer, and a good one.

Kareste spun on him. "I am an elùgroth. I serve no Kingshield Knight nor his underlings. I do not answer to Lindercroft, nor less to you. Remember that and live!"

She towered above him, and her eyes flashed. It was a trick she had learned, and she used it well. She allowed a touch of lòhrengai to shine in her eyes.

The captain took a step back, but he did not turn away. She had instilled fear in him; now it was time to induce trust.

"But have no fear. Serve me as you serve Lindercroft, and all will be well. For a time, his needs and mine match. The wizard must die, and then the boy and the girl are yours to hand over to the knight. They are all down there," and she pointed with her staff toward the bottom of the valley. "Down there, and fearful of what I will do when I catch them."

"Why didn't the knight tell us you were coming?"

There it was again. Mistrust. But at least he spoke civilly.

"The world turns swiftly, now. A great power rises in Faladir, and it calls and beckons to its own kind. You have seen the elù-drak, and no doubt other things. Now, you have seen an elùgroth. Lindercroft serves what we all do, and we all have tasks. His and mine match for a time. It would serve you well to contemplate what that task was. The better you understand that, the higher you will rise in the new world that is birthing."

She pulled her cowl even tighter. It was a dismissal, and the captain took it that way. He did not press matters further. And just as well. The answer she had given was no answer at all. But it had misdirected him and turned his thoughts to the future, and what prosperity he might gain from it. She just hoped his thoughts stayed there, at least for a while.

She led them on, moving downhill and ever deeper into the valley. Of old, a civilization had existed here, and there were still signs left for those who knew how to look. Even the path she chose now was once a road, and here and there were still exposed paving stones that once zigzagged from the very bottom of the valley to the top. Carts and people had followed that ancient road. But they were all gone now.

Yet something still remained. The road had led to a series of mines at the lowest point of the valley. At least, the lowest point above water level. She had explored them once, long ago, and that knowledge would help her now.

She swung back to face the men. "Get a supply of dry branches as you walk. You'll need them shortly."

They were close now. She did not explain her command to the men. That was not the elùgroth way, and though these men did not really know that, while they were wondering what use they would have for torches they were not wondering who she was.

Soon they came to a flat area, all tumbled rock and stunted trees. There were several mine entrances close by, if she remembered rightly.

A few moments later she saw what she was looking for. She glanced around at the men. They had gathered the branches as she had ordered.

"Good, you will need them. Light them up, and be quick about it."

Once more her tone was imperious. Really, she rather enjoyed playing the part she was. But the captain approached again, and that disturbed her.

"Where are we going? Why do we need torches in daylight?"

"No wonder you were fooled by an illusion," she said. "You can't even see what's before your face." She pointed at a brush-covered hollow close by. "Have a look there, and tell me what you see. Tread carefully."

The captain did as she commanded. He stamped down some bushes and cleared away brushwood until he exposed a vertical shaft. Then he stood back, looking at it dubiously.

"You can't mean for us to go down there?"

Kareste laughed. "Oh, but I do. Have no fear though, I shall go with you."

"It doesn't look safe," he said.

"It isn't." That, she had learned herself, but with due care no one was likely to die. "It's your choice," she told him. "That's where the enemy is. I intend to kill the wizard. The boy and the girl are nothing to me, so I'm not going to waste my time on them. If you want them, alive or dead, you'll have to come along."

She struck her staff against the ground, and light flared at its tip. Without hesitation, she moved to the shaft and lowered herself down. The others would follow, or not. She could not make them, but she had given them reason enough. She hoped they would, for Aranloth needed just a little bit more time to make his escape. He was encumbered by the young man with him. By himself, he could move faster and farther and did not need to rest. At least, he could use magic to sustain himself and put the need for rest off.

As she descended, she thought of the young man. What was he doing with Aranloth? Or better yet, what was Aranloth doing with him? For some reason, the old man had taken him under his protection. But why?

That Lindercroft pursued him was certain. But what interest did a Kingshield Knight have in finding and killing a young village man, she could not guess. But she had been close enough at times to hear some of his men, and she knew that was their mission.

The young man himself was troubling. He seemed so ordinary, and yet there was something in his gaze that was unsettling. He was not old, but she saw a strength of will in him that perhaps he had not even discovered himself yet. But it was there. He was the type that would ask a mountain to move, and if it did not he would set to work with a shovel and move it himself. No matter how long it took.

The shaft she descended was not quite vertical. And there were shallow steps carved in the stone to give her booted feet purchase. Slowly, step by careful step, she lowered herself until she came to the horizontal shaft she knew was there.

There she stood in the semi dark, her heart pounding. But soon someone followed her down. It was likely the captain, for he was a leader who went first and commanded the respect of his men. She almost liked him, and perhaps it was not his fault that he had ended up following orders from the knight.

She moved a little way ahead to make room for those who followed. The tunnel was narrow, for digging a mine like this was hard and dangerous work. Likely, the original miners had been after gold or silver. Only something like that would have justified the risk and expense.

The soldiers gathered behind her, muttering uncomfortably in the dark and confining space. But it was much lighter. They had lit their torches, but only some of them, keeping a supply in case needed later. That was very wise of them.

It was time to move. To wait longer was to risk conversation, and that she did not want. Lifting her staff a little higher, she stepped ahead along the narrow path. It was now filled with smoke, which she did not like. But the light was an improvement, for she had no love of narrow underground spaces. The men who had mined here were tough men, and men of courage. She admired them, but the sooner she got out of here the better. This was no place for her, and no place for the soldiers shuffling behind. But if all went well, they would have to endure this place longer than she did. That, at least, was the plan.

The going was difficult. The mining had been carried out over a long time, probably centuries, and the skill of the men who did it, or the willingness of various rulers to spend, fluctuated. This meant the tunnels themselves fluctuated. At times, she was forced to crawl on hand and foot to pass through low chambers. This, she did not like. It was not dignified to crawl ahead like this, with men watching her from behind.

Nothing was of any importance though, except that she had helped Aranloth. She had given him the time he needed now, and it was time for her to leave these men behind. They had torches. They knew the way they had come in, and so they could get out again. She had not lured them to their deaths here, though Lindercroft would be displeased with them when they finally reported back. He would be more dangerous to them than the mines.

The ceiling grew suddenly taller, and she was able to stand again.

"How much farther?" the captain asked. He was close behind her. Too close.

"Nearly there," she said. "Prepare your men."

As they were getting ready she moved ahead a few paces. This was the place she remembered. It was a crossroads, and various tunnels branched off at different angles. Some of these eventually led to the surface. The one to the left did so quickly, but the soldiers did not know that, and so long as they did not see which way she went they would be forced to retrace their route coming in here.

With a word of power, and a stamp of her staff on the stony ground, she drew on the powers of the earth and the air. Dust rose like a mist from the ancient floor, and a sudden howling wind drove it into the faces of the soldiers.

Kareste fled, darting down the left tunnel unseen, and in moments the yells and curses of the men grew faint and then were left behind.

She had made good her escape, but her task was not done yet. She must find Aranloth again and help him. Dark powers walked this part of the world, and the old man drew trouble to him like a flame drew moths. Lindercroft would learn of her interference and remember, but she would risk that, no matter how powerful the knights were becoming.

16. Older Than Faladir

Faran thought as he walked. Walking was good for that. Somehow, it freed the mind to wander.

Aranloth wanted to find some place where they were safe, and some way to throw the enemy off the trail. But was such a thing possible? The enemy was supported by creatures of the dark. How could they long evade something like an elù-drak? If there was one, there must be more. How could they dodge capture or killing with things such as that sent against them?

It was worrisome. Ferla had nearly died because of it. The old man was risking his life. The other lòhren, Kareste, risked hers as well. It had to end, and soon, or else someone *would* die.

"Where are we going?" he asked the old man, catching up to him as he strode up a long trail overshadowed by pines.

"Somewhere safe," the lòhren answered.

"But is there such a place? How long can we hide from the things that pursue us?"

The old man slowed. "What we do is dangerous. Our enemies make it so. But we should never give up hope. Never."

Faran thought on that. "I haven't given up hope."

"But you don't see a way forward?"

"No. I see no way out of this. Sooner or later Lindercroft will find us. Or me. After all, I seem to be the one he's really looking for."

Ferla shot him a hard look. "I know what you're starting to think. Don't! I won't let you."

Aranloth raised an eyebrow. "What is he thinking?"

"He's thinking the two of us are better off without him. He's thinking if he goes back and confronts Lindercroft, the two of us will be safe. He's thinking of trying to kill the knight and avenge our village."

The lòhren's second eyebrow rose. "You know him well, I see."

"I'm right here," Faran said. "There's no need to speak like I'm not even present."

"True enough, lad," Aranloth said. "So I'll say this directly to you, and I'll say it only once. If we wanted to leave you, we could. If Kareste did not want to help, she did not have to. All of us have had choices to make, and we made them. You have a choice to make, too. Several, in fact. But the biggest one right now is whether to live or die. If you faced Lindercroft now, he would kill you. He is not only a great warrior, but is also becoming a powerful sorcerer. It might just be that he has warded himself against the strike of arrows and the cut of blades. You would need magic to defeat him. And you have none. So, I'll assume you want to live, and that means following me."

The lòhren looked back uphill then, and quickened his pace. Ferla gave him a look as much as to say I told you so, and followed after. There was nothing for Faran to do but follow himself, but he was still unhappy about the situation.

Aranloth soon did something new though, and that diverted Faran's thoughts. The lòhren changed direction, and headed east. This would take them to the sea, and quickly.

Faran had never seen the sea before. But he had heard many stories. The city of Faladir was a city by the sea, and though Dromdruin had been farther inland, it was not by much. If they kept going in this direction they would come to the farthest shore of Alithoras swiftly. And as much as Faran wanted to see that, he was not sure why the lòhren would take them there. The ocean would block off a whole direction and limit their options to flee or hide. This was far from the city, and there would be no village nor boats there. At least, so far as he had ever heard.

The rest of the day passed without event. There was no sign of pursuit, but given the terrain that did not mean much. The enemy would be hard to see.

They had rested now and then for short whiles, and Aranloth kept a close eye on Ferla ensuring she was well enough to walk. She had recovered so well that few would have believed she had nearly died so recently. Even Aranloth seemed impressed.

They had stopped for the last time that day, or so Faran had thought. Dusk was settling over the land, but Aranloth stirred.

"I think we might be better off traveling through the night, now. Tonight, at least."

"What of the elù-drak?" Faran asked.

The old man glanced skyward. "In all things and in all decisions, there is risk. Lindercroft may have more than one in his service. Probably he has several. But who knows what else he has too? There are many creatures of the dark that the Morleth Stone might wake. Some are better hunters even than the elù-drak. Besides, you have seen one now and better know the dangers. And you have looked into the eyes of one and lived. That is rare. I think, if needs must, we can fight another one off."

The lòhren moved away then, using his staff as a walking stick, though he did not need to do so. Of them all, Faran now knew the lòhren could walk the swiftest and the farthest in a day.

They trailed after him. Faran was not sure the old man was right. They might not survive another attack from an elù-drak, and what if more than one came against them?

But he also sensed what he thought the old man feared. If they did not make an escape soon, Lindercroft would somehow find and pin them down. Then there would be more than just a dozen men to face.

The dark of night embraced them, and they trod wearily on. Just as during the day, Aranloth called frequent stops and rested. But these did not last long. And often the lòhren did not join them. He brooded away from where they sat, looking up into the night or into the dark folds of wooded land behind them. He must not have been able to see far, but then again Faran wondered if he always used sight. Could he reach out with magic and discern if they were followed?

Faran had no answers to his questions. He did not know enough about lòhrengai to even guess. He knew what legend said, but legends had a way of obscuring some truths and giving too much prominence to others. Aranloth himself was an example of that. It was said that he was the greatest of the lòhrens, their lord or king, if they had such a term for their leader. He was exalted, and yet he acted more or less the same now when his identity was revealed as he had as a vagabond healer wandering the land.

The night pressed in. The miles passed, and toward dawn the sound of the sea rose up. Faran had not heard it before, but he had heard it described. It was a kind of music. Immensely sad, yet resolute. It was the sound of the earth itself, and it had voiced its lament at the burden of existence long before the first person had walked its shores. And it would still be doing so long after its restless waters had washed away the last of their tracks into oblivion.

A keen breeze hit Faran's face, and despite his tiredness he felt alive. This was something new.

The noise of the waves grew louder, and as the first light of dawn grayed the sky they came to a stone staircase cut into cliffs, and the sea itself filled his vision. Vast it was, heaving, gray and somber. It filled his eyes and his ears and the cry of white-winged birds came distantly to him.

Faran looked to Ferla, and he saw that she was already looking at him, wonder in her eyes. The forest held both their hearts, but here was something they could love also.

Aranloth paused as well, but not for long. "Beware the stone. It'll be slippery with dew and sea spray." Holding his staff loosely in his right hand, he descended the stairs.

Faran breathed in of the tangy air, and then he and Ferla walked down behind the lòhren. The staircase was not wide, but it was wide enough that they could descend side by side. This they did, and they did not talk. They each knew what the other was thinking, and there was no need for words.

Aranloth had been right. The stone was wet and dangerous. But the staircase was well crafted, if ancient and crumbling. It was steep in places, and in others it curved out following the line of the cliffs where there was a bulge. Turning and twining, at last it led them down to the shore.

The noise of the white-winged birds was louder here, and they hovered and banked in the shifting airs.

"Seagulls," Aranloth told him, seeing his curiosity.

Faran noticed that they weren't really white-winged. Their bodies were white, and the underneath of their wings, but the top side was gray.

"That stairway was old," Ferla said. "You could see where the walking of people over long years had worn a hollow into the middle of each step."

Aranloth nodded. "Very old. Older even than Faladir. But Faladir is a young city."

That was something to think about. Faran had heard the legends of its founding, and that's what they were to him. Stories and legends from the deeps of time. If that was a young city, then what would the lòhren call an old one?

Aranloth led them along the shore as daylight grew. At one place he paused, jutting out the tip of his staff to point with.

"Look there," he said.

Faran saw what he meant. Shimmering below the water he saw straight lines of stone. It seemed to be some sort of sunken city, though he was not sure if he was looking at roads or tumbled buildings.

"The sea has changed over the long years," the lòhren told his companions. "It has risen, and it has swallowed a once great city. There lie the remains of Arach Nedular, an ancient port. Once, the white-sailed ships outnumbered the seagulls. Here, were splendid parties that ran all night where the red wines of Darr-harran flowed like water in rivers. Here, women in bejeweled dresses danced with men who never wore swords and where even the dock workers dressed in silks. But they are all gone now. Mud beneath the waves, and the ancient world is nothing but a fleeting memory."

A moment longer the lòhren held out his staff, his face unreadable. Then he shuffled forward, for once looking like the old man that he was.

Faran exchanged a look with Ferla. "He is *so* old," she said. "What has he lost in his lifetime? How many has he known and loved that are gone like the city?"

It was a question that Faran could not answer. He was too young to understand, and he knew it. And he was scared of getting old enough that it would one day make sense.

They walked in the old man's tracks. Close behind him, but a world apart at the same time.

The tide had gone out. Faran knew little of such things, but he thought it was coming in again. The sea seemed to be getting closer anyway. Maybe that was why Aranloth seemed unconcerned about leaving such a clear trail behind them.

A flicker of movement caught Faran's eye behind them. He turned to look, and saw a figure on the stone stairs, far behind.

Ferla hissed through her teeth. She had seen it too, but the figure was obscured now by some twist of the stairs.

"We must hurry!" she said, catching up to the lòhren. "There's a—"

"I know," Aranloth said. But he seemed unperturbed. Maybe he was still overcome by the great sadness that seemed to have settled over him.

Not long after, the shore swung around an outjutting section of cliffs. They towered above, grim, slicked by dew and crusted with ancient lichens. There was no winding staircase here. But there was a cave. And before it, a stele.

"What *is* this place?" Faran asked, filled with a sense of unease.

The lòhren seemed lost in thought. He leaned on his staff and gazed at the stele.

"Not all that the ancients built is lost. This is one such place. But what is it? Hopefully, to us, safety. We will see."

Faran did not like the look of it. The cave was unsettling, as though something dwelt within. And the stele had writing on it, but of a sort that he had never seen and could not read.

And Aranloth himself was unsettling. He had seemed lost in the past now for a while, but it was the present he should be concentrating on. That figure, whoever it was, would have seen them and even now be catching up quickly.

17. A Place of Power

The lòhren seemed to have lost all sense of danger at their situation. He continued talking as though there was no pursuit.

"The ancients worshipped at places of power," he said. "And there are many such, spread out across the land. Often they are in caves, and usually there is water."

Whoever that figure was that followed them, it must be close now. And then Faran heard the tread of feet on sand. He notched an arrow to his bow, and prepared to draw.

"You'll not need that, lad."

The lòhren's voice was focused once more, and confident to boot. But Faran had been followed too long, and too much had happened for him to put down his weapon.

And yet as the figure came into view, he did. It was the other lòhren.

Aranloth, for once, did not lean on his staff. He leaned against the stele instead.

"Well met, Kareste," he offered by way of greeting as she drew up to them.

"If you say so, old man."

It was a strange response, but there was a smile on her face and joy in her eyes that told the opposite story of her words.

Faran saw that she looked just as she had before, only now her robes were white and her cloak was brown instead of black, and the staff in her hands was not wychwood but a honey-colored timber.

Kareste's gaze fell on him, and he felt the weight of her consideration. Then it was gone, like a cloud drifting away and allowing the sun to shine once more. That gaze had seemed to see straight through him, to know who and what he was, what he would say and do, and how he would think and feel about it better even than he did.

"What happened with the soldiers?" Aranloth asked.

She grinned at him. "I led them on a merry dance, taking them to the old mines at the bottom of the valley."

"Ah, and that's where you left them?"

"Yes, and they'll still be cursing me. Can't say as I blame them, but it was better than killing them. They'll have gotten out and reported to Lindercroft by now. They won't thank me for that, either."

Faran was surprised. "You mean to say you left us, went back down to the bottom of the valley and then caught up with us again?"

Kareste glanced momentarily at Aranloth, and then back to him.

"I'm a quick walker," she replied. But having spoken to him, her attention remained fixed on him again, and it did not waver. "Who are you?"

"My name is Faran," he answered.

"And what are you doing with…"

Her voice trailed away, but Aranloth spoke up. "They know my name."

She raised an eyebrow at that. "Well then? What are you doing with Aranloth?"

"He knew my grandfather, and we met in Dromdruin village after—"

"I see," she said, interrupting him, and Faran did not mind. He had no wish to explain what had happened. But she seemed to know all about it anyway.

"I went there," she said softly, and then she looked at Aranloth. "I was trying to track you down, but I was too late. I had not really believed that the knights had fallen, but they have done so. And dark things walk the land and fly the skies."

"We know," Ferla said. "We've met them. One at least."

Kareste nodded at that. "I see. The shadow of fear is still upon you. It's in your eyes."

"Well it might be," Aranloth said. "Ferla was poisoned by an elù-drak."

The green-brown eyes of Kareste widened. "And she still lives? Few have ever survived that."

"I wouldn't have," Ferla said. "But Faran saved me."

Those eyes turned to him again, and there was speculation in them.

"I sent him on the Paths of the Dead," Aranloth told her. "He alone knew Ferla well enough to bring her back."

Kareste whistled at that. "Well now, you're no ordinary young man, that's all I can say."

She glanced at Aranloth, and Faran saw something unsaid pass between them. But the old man appeared done talking on that subject.

"We've spent enough time catching up on things. You led Lindercroft's men away and gained us some time. We'd better make the most use of that."

Kareste nodded thoughtfully, and pointed with her staff at the cave entrance.

"A good choice," she said. "It's how I found you though, thinking you would come here. Lindercroft might think likewise."

"Perhaps, but there was nowhere else."

They walked into the shadow of the cave, and immediately the two lòhrens raised their staffs. Light glowed at their tips, and the dark interior was partially revealed.

The floor was of sand, and it was wet. At high tide, which could not be far away now, the sea would enter here. That was to the good, for it might help hide them or slow anyone down who knew where they were and tried to follow. Faran put that from his mind though. With two lòhrens to help them now, surely they must be safe?

Aranloth did not hesitate. He led the way, and he took them to the back of the cave, and turned left where the walls narrowed and offered several smaller openings. Each looked like black pits into the unknown to Faran, but obviously not so to the lòhren. He had been here before, and knew the way.

The left cave was quite narrow, and they walked in single file, though they did not have to duck their heads. It did not take Faran long to work out that this was not actually a cave. Perhaps it had been so for a little while at the beginning, but it ran too straight and too true. Also, by the steady light of the lòhren's staffs, he saw the marks of chisels in stone.

They did not talk. Aranloth led, Faran and Ferla followed, and Kareste took up a guard position in the rear. Perhaps it was only so that the light of the staffs was spread out, but Faran felt in his bones it was not so. From time to time, he saw her look behind them, and perhaps even strain to listen for any indications that they were being followed.

The tunnel ceased abruptly. At least, it appeared to. But there was a hole in the ground, round and smooth. Aranloth let himself down through this, and they followed.

It was only a short drop to the bottom, perhaps less than five feet. There, they crawled for a dozen feet or so on hands and knees. It was not a good feeling to be deep underground and crawling. The thought of all the stone in the cliffs above made Faran nervous, but soon the narrow space widened and they were in a tunnel again. This one was wide though. All four of them could walk abreast, and the walls were smooth and true as though built by a master craftsman. Faran supposed they were. The ancients were reputed to be great builders, and they had spent time and effort here. Although he could not fathom why the earlier parts of the tunnel were so rough or the purpose of the hole they had let themselves down. Maybe it was some sort of defensive plan. For surely, had they wanted to, they could have delved all the tunnels just like this one.

Aranloth led them swiftly now, and though they walked abreast they did not talk. The first few times that either Faran or Ferla tried to, their whispers echoed strangely and came back to them as a sibilant hiss that they did not like. It seemed to Faran that this place did not wish the presence of humans. Maybe that was fanciful, but he ceased making any attempt at conversation.

In near silence they walked, but there was one sound. As though from a great distance they heard the slow rise and fall of the sea. And here and there, they came to staircases crafted out of the naked stone of the earth, and descending these the sound of water became stronger.

"I smell the sea," Ferla whispered. And the walls threw her voice back at her.

Aranloth slowed and answered, yet when he did so he somehow pitched his voice so that there was no echo.

"We come now to a dangerous place. Walk carefully. Do not tarry. And keep your eyes fixed on the floor. To fall might be to die."

It was not reassuring. Faran began to wonder if it had been a mistake to come here, and that perhaps they might have been better off outside. But it was too late now.

Aranloth led them down another spiral of stairs, and Faran noticed that the stone was wet. Then the tunnel opened up. A great lake lay before them. But then soon

Faran realized it was no lake, but the sea itself. It rose and fell to the same rhythm that it did outside.

The chamber was vast, and it seemed as though it was a thing of nature and not crafted by people. Yet people had added to what nature had made.

The water tossed and swirled in the center. To the left were great carvings in the stone. Men and women. Kings with crowns and queens with bright diadems. There were others too. Perhaps priests, and these were depicted with staffs, and there were farmers and soldiers as well.

Faran had never seen anything like it. But the lòhren led them to the right. Here a platform was carved into the wall, halfway up to the ceiling. It was narrow, wide enough for only one person at a time.

"Watch where you walk," the lòhren warned again, and he stepped onto the platform.

As they had done before, Aranloth led, followed by Faran and Ferla with Kareste coming up behind. The stone beneath their boots was slick, and the walls crusted with salt.

They had gone perhaps a third of the way when the water below seethed and roiled. A roaring filled Faran's ears, but he still heard Aranloth yell.

"Crouch down and press yourself against the wall!"

Faran did so, and only just in time.

The water heaved and bubbled, then it gushed up in a mighty wave and crashed against the wall. It drove at Faran, and had he been standing or caught unprepared, he would have fallen.

But then the water dropped down again, swirling and thrashing as it retreated. He was soaking wet, but strangely he heard Kareste laugh behind him. He glanced back at her, and those green-brown eyes were dancing. Ferla looked somewhat less happy, and her red hair was dripping.

"Carefully now!" Aranloth called. "Let's go before another wave comes."

He stood up then, and walked once more, but slower than before. Faran understood why immediately. The footing was even more treacherous than it had been. Water slicked the stone like oil in a cooking pot, and each step was a gamble against death.

And death it would be to fall into the roiling water below. A man would drown there no matter how well he could swim.

He glanced at the water, and wished he had not. Fear gripped him, but he felt Ferla's hand on his shoulder from behind. Yet even as that reassured him, he saw something that set his heart leaping.

Down in the water was a woman, yet while it swirled about her, covering her, she remained motionless. And her eyes fixed on his. Then the water foamed, and when it cleared, she was not there.

Faran stumbled ahead. It was not possible. He had imagined it. Yet it had seemed so clear to see, if but just for a moment.

They came to the other side. The platform widened and led into another wide tunnel. This one climbed upward.

Aranloth waited for them, unaffected by the peril they had just passed through. He looked as though he had merely walked over a few stepping stones on a garden path, but he saw Faran and his eyes narrowed.

"What is it, lad? You're whiter than milk in a black bucket. Do you have a fear of heights?"

Faran shook his head.

"Then what is it? Something troubles you."

"I thought I saw a lady. A lady in the water."

Aranloth leaned on his staff. He seemed the picture of quietness and calm, but there was a flicker of hidden interest in his eyes.

"What of you?" he said, turning to Ferla and Kareste.

They had seen nothing, as Faran knew they would not have. But he knew also that he had seen what he had seen, even if they had not.

The old man shrugged. "Perhaps you imagined it. Or maybe not. As I said earlier, this is a place of power, and the ancients came to this very spot. They worshiped here, and they sought guidance here in times of need. It is said, every once in a while, perhaps once in a century, that a lady rose from the water and answered their questions."

Faran thought on that. "She is real, then?"

"I did not say that."

"But you don't deny it, either."

The old man grinned at him. "No, I don't. The world is full of many strange things, and many powers beyond our knowledge. Who is to say what is truth and what is superstition?"

It seemed the old man would say no more though, for he turned and led them on again quickly. Faran walked after him, but not before he saw those green-brown eyes of Kareste weigh him up again like a horse-trader buying a breeding stallion.

Aranloth led them quickly after that. And this was despite the fact that caves turned to tunnels and tunnels turned to caves, and they climbed stairs and descended hollows in the rock. Their path was a maze, and apparently one only Aranloth knew.

"The enemy will not follow us through here," he said. "Even if they dared to enter at all."

The lòhren seemed confident, but despite this Faran noticed that he led them at times through shallow pools of water to hide their trail.

They walked through one such pool, and though the water was shallow where they trod over a kind of causeway, on either side it quickly deepened and there Faran glimpsed strange creatures swimming through the water.

"Sea snakes," Kareste told him. "Deadly if they bite you."

That sent a chill up his spine, and yet they were beautiful nonetheless, gliding and arcing with sublime grace beneath the water's surface.

They moved on from there, and then rested. Then moved on, and rested again. So it went, and Faran lost all sense of direction and of time. If not for Aranloth, there would be no chance of finding a way back out again.

It was a strange world down here, beneath the rock of the cliffs. Part of it was fashioned by the hands of humans, and the walls were smooth or carved with decorations. Other parts were natural. In these, Faran sensed something. It was a presence. It was a feeling the same as he had when he saw the lady beneath the water in the great pool.

Kareste seemed to notice what he felt after a while. It was no surprise, those green-brown eyes were always studying him.

"You sense the magic," she said. Although whether it was a question or a statement he was not sure.

They moved on, and it seemed now that they began to move upward.

There was no real sense of time, just of weariness. The stairs took their toll on his legs, for some were long and steep. But they came at length to a smooth shaft that at some point turned from a carved tunnel to a natural cave, though it was hard to tell exactly when the transition occurred.

After a little while, they walked on rubble. Part of the roof had collapsed, but ahead came a glow of light. They had reached the outside world again.

The light from the lòhren's staffs faded away, and the travelers emerged carefully from the depths of the earth to a green headland, facing the sea. Noon had come and passed, but there were still hours of daylight to go.

Faran enjoyed the fresh air of the sea blowing on his face, and he was surprised that they had not been underground longer. He was glad, but not surprised, that there was no sign of the enemy. They had surely lost them, for no one could know where they had exited the caves.

"Well, what do we do now?" he asked.

18. A Dead Man

Aranloth seemed about to speak, but Kareste spoke first.

"I have some news," she said. "Inside the caves was not the time to share it, but now it is."

For a just a moment, her gaze flickered to Faran and he knew it concerned him. But it was Aranloth she spoke to.

"When I led the soldiers astray, I learned several things. They thought I was there to help, so they spoke freely."

"And what did you learn?" Aranloth asked.

"This, and it isn't good. Lindercroft had over a hundred men in service to him for his … mission. But since it failed, he has sent for reinforcements. A thousand new soldiers are on the way, and there's a price on Faran's head."

Faran had known something bad was coming, but that still shocked him. He kept his voice steady though when he spoke.

"What price did they put on me?"

Kareste studied him. "They say you can judge a man by his enemies. I've always believed that was true. And you have some serious enemies. The man to kill you, or take you to Lindercroft, will earn the weight of your head in gold."

Faran felt a chill creep into his very bones. How was any of this even possible? He was a hunter from Dromdruin village – nothing more and nothing less. Now a Kingshield Knight had put a price on his head. Maybe even the king himself had ordered it. It was all impossible, but even so, he did not doubt Kareste's words. But he thought he might be sick.

"I cannot be the seventh knight. I *will* not be the seventh knight."

For all that his insides were a seething mess, those words came out strong and true. He meant them, as he had seldom meant anything before.

The old man looked at him kindly. If he were disappointed or annoyed at that response, he kept those feelings hidden. But he did have an opinion on the matter, and he shared it.

"This is what you have to consider. You're being backed into a corner, but not by me. I know what you wish. I know it better than anyone. People know who I am. They call me Aranloth the Lòhren. Or Aranloth the White. They call me many things, but never do they stop to think if I asked for those things. I wanted none of them. Circumstances drove me—"

"Nothing will make me become a Kingshield Knight," Faran interrupted. "I hate them for what they did to my grandfather. Nothing will ever change that."

Aranloth shrugged. "That's not what I was trying to convince you of. But no matter. This is the point. What I believe and what you believe don't matter here. It's what Lindercroft believes that counts."

"What do you mean?"

"I mean that whether or not you're meant to be the seventh knight doesn't matter. And even if you are the seventh knight, you can refuse your destiny. But Lindercroft? Well, he's not going to take any chances. So far as he's concerned, you *might* be a threat. For the possibility alone, he'll do all he can to kill you."

That hit Faran like a punch in the belly. It was truth, and he knew it. Lindercroft cared nothing for what he would or would not do. All that mattered to him was what his enemy *might* do. And Lindercroft was the type to kill his enemies.

For the first time, Faran realized he was a dead man. No matter where he went or what he did.

"Perhaps none of it matters," he said. "I'll not become the seventh knight, but that doesn't mean I won't kill Lindercroft for what he's done. The massacre of an entire village demands justice."

Kareste pulled her cloak close about her, and took a firm grip on her staff.

"Very touching, I'm sure. But now isn't the time to think of justice. It's a time to think of survival. We've escaped them, for now. They'll find us again though. What we need to do is make a plan to escape."

Aranloth nodded. "That's what we must do. All else will follow from that."

He began to discuss their options with Kareste, but Faran had no interest in it, nor did he know these lands and where best they could go to try to hide.

Ferla came to his side and put an arm around his shoulder.

"Let's give them a chance to work something out," she said, and she led him a little way away where they sat down on an outcrop of rock. There, they did not talk. Nor did she take her arm away. They sat quietly, and looked out toward the sea.

Gray and vast, the sea rolled and glittered before them. Seagulls and other birds rode the winds. The sun began to fall, and it sent shards of light to break and splinter amid the cresting waves.

Faran felt empty. He had a mission, though it was not his destiny and he had no ability to fulfill it. He had a destiny, perhaps, but he disowned it. And well he should. If the Kingshield Knights had fallen, then they did not need a new and seventh knight. Let them slip into oblivion like so many other things before them. Their time was done.

The sun did not fall much farther before Ferla nudged him.

"They've reached a decision," she said.

Faran looked over. The two lòhrens were walking toward him.

19. We Fear Nothing

Lindercroft sat cross-legged, the metal of his calf and thigh greaves and the loose stones of the cave floor digging into his flesh.

He was not comfortable, but pain was to be endured. He had been a Kingshield Knight, and was now become something new. Something Alithoras had not seen before. Pain was a spur to action. Mistakes were the foundation of success. The discomfort of reprimand a ladder to future greatness.

And reprimand he was expecting. It could not be otherwise. He did not look forward to it. He did not fear it. He was a knight, and what did not break him made him stronger as a weapon of the new world order that was coming.

He sat still, breathing deep. Not to his chest, but to his abdomen. There he concentrated, focusing on the *harharat*, the center of being two finger-widths below his navel.

The feel of his naked sword across his thighs was acknowledged, but ignored. The lingering smell of smoke in the air from the fire that had gone out was noted, and then dismissed. That Aranloth had hid in this very cave with the boy, and then escaped, chagrined him, but he let that go.

The men outside had fires. But he must be alone to do what had to be done next. As a knight, he stood apart and above ordinary men. He must endure discomfort and hardship with a calm mind. So too must he channel pain as a force to focus the mind.

It was time, and he was prepared. He uttered the words of power, and they rebounded to him from the walls of the cave. The men outside had been warned not to come in, and it was death for them if they did. By magic or steel. Or both.

He followed the ritual as it had been taught to him, but not by *Osahka* – the guide. He felt a momentary lapse in concentration. The guide was revered, for he had overseen their order since the beginning. No, he was the enemy. He was to be opposed, and even killed if possible. His name was Aranloth, and no guide was needed now. The new order of knights went their own way, where and how they would. They had outgrown their guide, outgrown the rules of men and the restraints of humanity.

Leaving the naked sword rest across his thighs, he did not move it at all. Rather, he ran the palm of his left hand along its middle portion, and pressed.

The cold steel cut. Aranloth was forgotten, and memories of him. Pain flooded through him, and he used this to focus his mind. *Pain was to be endured.*

He clenched his hand, which sent a deeper stab of pain up his arm, but he paid it no heed. He was a knight, and earthly pain was as distant as his long-forgotten memories.

For five long breaths, he kept his hand clenched, feeling the blood pool and gather. On the sixth breath, he raised the clenched fist, opened it, and smeared the blood over his forehead.

Immediately, he felt the magic. Blood magic. His arm trembled at it, but he ignored it. Like a man waking from sleep, slowly his consciousness grew. He had woken the *olek-nas*, the third eye, which was a level of the mysteries that he could not achieve under the guidance of Aranloth. Yet with the new ways of the knights, all things were possible.

Now, he could see the real world and also the hidden world. The world of spirit. The realm of magic. Pride surged through him, and he stifled it. Pride was a sin. Pride was for lesser men. The great achieved great deeds, and let other men marvel at them while they moved on to yet a greater deed still.

He let his mind drift, and it found the currents of magic that connected him to the king, and through the king to the Morleth Stone.

His vision sharpened. His spirit eyes saw with increasing clarity.

The king sat upon his throne. It was not the old throne of the kings of ages past. It was new, as was fitting for the greatest king in the history of Faladir. It was wrought of steel, blackened to the color of jet, and inlaid with crimson. Words of power were engraved upon it, and enchantments laid over it. But the magic of the king was stronger by far.

Lindercroft gazed at him. The man was old. Too old to be a knight, and yet his face was flushed with youth and strength and skill was in his arms. Oldest of the knights, he remained yet the fastest and most skillful with a sword. None could defeat him with a practice sword, and none would dare raise a steel blade against him.

His hair was white. Once, it had been black, and Lindercroft remembered those days, and the days after when it was shot through with gray. But overnight, it seemed, gray had transformed to white.

Lindercroft did not look into his eyes. But he knew they were piercing as driven nails, even if bloodshot.

The king's long hair spilled gracefully down beneath a silver crown. This was the crown of old that all kings had worn, but none had worn it with as much power as this.

Crimson robes flowed down over the black throne, but here and there beneath them Lindercroft saw the armor of a knight. The king wore armor always these days. Enemies were everywhere, he said, and he was right.

Those bloodshot eyes turned to him, and even though Lindercroft did not meet their gaze, he felt the force of the will behind them.

The king did not greet him. That would not be fitting.

"Hail, Your Majesty," Lindercroft said.

The king studied him for a moment. "What news, Lindercroft. Is the boy dead yet?"

Lindercroft sensed eagerness behind the simple question, and he had no wish to give this man bad news.

"Aranloth has come, as we feared," he answered. Perhaps that might deflect blame, but this was unlikely.

The king gazed at him silently a long moment. "What of it? He is an old man, and weaker now than us. Nor, as you put it, do we fear him. We are Morleth Knights, and we fear nothing. Is that not so?"

"It is so."

"Then why do I sense fear? Come, Lindercroft. I am your master, and you have nothing to fear from me. Now speak. The boy is not dead yet. Say the words."

"He is not dead, yet. But I know his name now, and I am seeking him out."

Lindercroft told of the raid on Dromdruin valley, and of the killings there. He spoke succinctly, missing no important detail, but reporting events as they had occurred. He told of how he still felt uneasy, for they had never divined the exact identity of who may become the seventh knight, and he had decided to spirit-fly the land. By chance, he saw Aranloth. He told of his meeting with the lòhren, and the boy who might be the seventh. Aranloth had tried to hide it, but it was clear that he believed him so, and he was under his protection. He told of the failure of his men, and that he had summoned more for the search. All the while, the cold eyes of the king gazed at him, and searched his soul for the truth or any sign of deceit.

He would find no deceit.

Lindercroft fell silent. A long while the king sifted his words, and did not break the quiet.

"You call the enemy a boy," he said at length. "But rather, is he not a young man? And you make no mention of the girl with him?"

"Your Majesty – he seems as but a boy to me, but yes, he is a young man. And the girl is of no consequence."

The king leaned forward on his dark throne. "The two of them somehow evaded your men in Dromdruin, and that was before the lòhren helped them. The girl defied an elù-drak to save the boy, and the boy spirit walked the Paths of the Dead to bring her home. No, these are not boys and girls. Whoever they are, they're a threat to us. Kill them. Kill them both."

Lindercroft bowed his head. There was much in the king's words that he had not known. It was best not to forget the man had acquired mysterious powers greater than the other knights. Yet still, how had he learned things of the enemy that he himself, in close pursuit, had not known?

The king spoke again, his voice a whisper drifting on the spirit winds.

"Is the young man the one we truly seek?"

Uncertainty washed over Lindercroft. It was a feeling that he disliked.

"He may be."

"And you have failed to kill him, as you were charged to do?"

"He is not dead yet, but that will be remedied shortly."

The king sat back on his throne. "You disappoint me. You seek to evade my question."

Lindercroft bowed his head. "I am at fault, Your Majesty. It pains me, but I have failed in my primary mission. Yet I will redress that error swiftly. I still hunt the youth, and we are closing in. I will find him, and I will kill him. Personally. Nothing will stop me."

The king gazed at him in silence. "I believe you," he said. "At least, I believe that you will remedy your error. Yet if our order is to rise, we must be the best of the best. Mistakes are for others, not us. You shame your brethren, and you shame me. Worse even than making the error, you still possess pride. It sings in your answer, and that must be purged from you."

Lindercroft knew it was so, yet the shadow of fear was upon him. He wondered if the other knights ever felt this also. Inadequate. Scared. Unfit for the great purpose fate had lifted them up to fulfil.

"You do not answer me, knight, and I know my words have found a weakness in you. You are too full of pride, and this is a sin. And we strive for virtue, do we not?"

"Yes, Your Majesty. We strive for virtue."

There was silence, heavy as a mountain, between the two men.

"Punish me, Your Majesty. It will spur me to be a better knight than I am."

The king did not answer. He gave no sign that he had heard, but he closed his eyes and Lindercroft braced himself. *Pain was to be endured.*

White-hot flame lashed his face, tearing skin, burning flesh and heating his eyes within his sockets until they boiled like eggs in a pot. He screamed; the demeanor of a knight stripped from him in a mere moment.

It was illusion. He knew it was illusion. But that made no difference. It *felt* real, and therefore it *was* real until the king relented.

Pain was to be endured! Lindercroft screamed that in his mind, though he no longer believed it. Yet still, moment by moment, he put into place the training of a knight.

The body felt pain. The mind controlled the body. The mind could leave the body, if it wished. The mind could perceive the body as something other, and the pain it felt could be as distant as the stars in the void from the blue earth.

This brought some relief. Tears streamed out of his eyes, and he knew they were still there. But even in thinking of his eyes his mind drew close to his body again, and he felt those tears turn to acid that ate away into his flesh, dissolving his face.

The king was inventive, and even as Lindercroft's mind turned away from the thought, a new agony struck him. The sword over his thighs turned to molten metal and dripped through flesh and into the marrow of his bones. He screamed again, and found the sweet mercy of oblivion.

When he woke, he forced himself up off the ground where he lay. The king still gazed at him.

"You are yet weak, Lindercroft."

Lindercroft sat cross-legged again. His body trembled and he could find no breath for answer.

"You are weak," the king said again, "but you will grow stronger. I will forge you into a great knight yet."

"Yes, Your Majesty," Lindercroft answered.

"You may continue your search for the two fugitives."

Lindercroft offered a shaky bow of his head. It was the best he could manage.

The bloodshot eyes of the king regarded him as an ordinary man might study an axeblade that he had just sharpened.

"Know this, though. I have already sent another hunter. One summoned through the power of the stone. Where you are weak, it is strong."

Lindercroft bowed once more, and when he looked up the king was fading, but still the gaze of those bloodshot eyes was heavy upon him. With a shudder, Lindercroft realized that such a creature could be sent for him one day, if he failed the king too often.

But he would fail no more. He stood, and pain stabbed through him. It was only the shadow of remembered pain, the lingering of the magic, yet it was still agony and would be so for hours. But it was nothing compared to what the boy would face when either of his hunters, man or summoned beast, found him.

20. Shadow Hunter

It knew its own name. Elùdurlik. It knew what that name meant. Shadow Hunter. It was one with the name, and then a new thought arose.

What was its purpose?

Even as the thought was born, the answer sparked to life within its mind. Its purpose was to hunt, to find and to kill.

To kill what?

Not all things, though it flexed its hand and sharp claws slid from their sheathes, and it knew that all things could be its rightful prey.

But that was not its true purpose. That was a means of sustenance only. A momentary joy. It could not compare with its reason for existence.

And it had one. A goal. A purpose. A motivation to draw breath.

Breath? It breathed deep of the air, and it knew it was a thing born of spirit and magic, but that it moved in a world of size, space and physical limits. It could breathe. And run. And hide. And kill. And it could…

Yes. It could taste. And it would taste. Blood. That would nourish it, but its purpose was to seek out and kill one being in particular.

It did not know who that was. It did not care. It did know how to find its trail and follow it. That knowledge was born into its mind even as strength was built into its legs.

It stood from where it had wakened on the ground. It stood on two legs. Hair covered them. Fur. But they were strong, and he felt them quiver with the need to run.

And Elùdurlik ran. Shadow Hunter was free of the spirit world, and part of the world of flesh. He ran, and he felt joy.

Shadow Hunter. He did not hunt shadows, he hunted *from* the shadows. A thrill ran through him, and he trembled at the feel of it.

Life. Magic had birthed him, and an image of a man, white-haired and powerful came to him. It had been his magic, but that was the past and it slipped from his mind.

All that mattered was the future. To feast on the blood of the one he hunted.

Elùdurlik sped through the dark. It was a forest. This he knew, but did not know how. Nor did he know how he knew a city, teeming with prey, lay close behind him.

The city was forbidden to him. But that was now. His mind wakened further, and he grasped that once he completed the task for which he was born, other tasks might await him. Perhaps, even in the city where the scent of blood was strong.

He ran on, twining through the trees like a shadow of the night, yet swift as the wind and silent as an owl on soft wings.

So much he knew, and it seemed to him that the world was young. He only had to think of something, and knowledge stirred to life. The white-haired man-thing was powerful in magic. He would never be prey. But all else might become so.

Thirst. Hunger. These were new also. Shadow-hunter did not like them. Not all in this world was good. And yet the quenching of thirst would be sweet, and the satiating of hunger fulfilling.

He sped on. The night grew dark about him, but he was darker still. At times, he fell down to lope on four legs. This was good. He could scent the ground better that way, but he could not run so fast and see ahead of him so well. Two-legs was better.

The miles were eaten by his feet. It was not nourishment-food, but it was still satisfying. He was strong. He could run fast. He felt like he could run forever, and that was good.

A new scent. Time had passed. His feet had eaten mile after mile. He slowed and thought.

Smoke. Fire. No, that was not quite right. Old-smoke. Old-fire. Things that had lived in a frenzy and then died.

Death. He came to a stop. That thought was profound. Death. The end of all things. Or the beginning? He had come from nothing. If he returned to nothing, might he yet be born again?

This was too much. He thought thoughts, but no answers came. He howled into the air, and felt fear quicken through the forest. He was alive. He would not die. No need to trouble himself with birth and death. He *was*, and that was all that mattered.

He entered a valley, and excitement quickened through his veins. This was the place. Here, he would find the trail of the one he hunted. He knew it, as he knew so many other things.

Like the shadow of a cloud drifting over the land, he passed through the forest and found a road. The smell of man-thing was strong here, but he ignored it. The man-things had been everywhere. Back and forth for days and weeks. He could scent it all, but it was hard to separate them out.

He went down on all four legs, loping again and scenting the ground better. Soon. It would be soon now.

The village reeked of old-smoke and old-fire when he found it. And death.

It did not take him long. He found a new road, once inside the group of two-leg dwelling places. Scents were everywhere, but there he found the scent of a magic-man. Like, but also unlike his white-haired father.

Father? It was so. White-hair had called him into being and given him purpose. That purpose had begun now. Magic-man had met two others at this spot. Magic-man had left, and the two two-legs with him. These were his prey. He knew them now, and all the world could turn and slide into oblivion before he forgot them. But first-prey was the young male two-legs. He would die first. The others in their turn, but first-prey was the one.

Shadow Hunter rose up on his own two-legs and howled. He stretched up with his other legs. No. Arms. Arms when he stood upright, but legs when he loped. Yes. He stretched up, and his claws slid from their sheathes. He was Shadow Hunter, and the world would tremble at his presence.

He bounded ahead, following the trail that now he could never lose. The hunt had begun, and the taste of blood was at its end.

Loping and scenting the ground, he pursued his quarry. The scent was old. But moons would have to pass before it grew so old that it could not be detected.

Water. He did not like it. He hated it. Cold and wet. Treacherous. It tried to hide the scent from him. No. That was not right. It was magic-man. Clever-magic-man. He used the water as a tool to hide his passing.

Clever. Frustrating. But Shadow Hunter is great. Shadow Hunter clever also. The scent was still there, below the surface of the water. Faint. Very faint. But he could follow it still.

He moved slowly now. Sometimes he went on four-legs to better smell. Sometimes he stood on two-legs, to better think like a man-thing and consider how and where he would have moved in their place.

Through water and over rocks and up hills and down hills he followed. Sometimes fast, and sometimes slow. But he did not lose the trail.

Hunger. Tiredness. He did not like them, but he recognized their cause. He needed food. He needed sleep. Then he would take up the hunt again.

It did not take him long to scent food. Four-foots were close by. What white-hair called deer.

He left behind the trail of first-prey. He would come back to it. Like a shadow he moved over the land, moving slowly and silently. This was stalking, and he liked it as much as following a trail.

The deer were not hard to find. But they were wary. Yes, they were wary and cautious. This was good. It was not fitting to hunt easy prey.

Fitting? Fairness? These were man-thoughts. He dismissed them. Moving silently, he came around and approached a herd of deer. He made sure the breeze blew toward him. They would not scent him that way. Nor would they see him. He was Shadow Hunter.

He came close. He sensed their nervousness. They were wary, and though they could not know he was there, yet still something warned them.

Even as they wheeled to run away, he ran and leaped. The pursuit did not last long. He was fast. He knew that he could run all day, but now he knew also that he was faster than deer.

His claws raked across the hind's back. Blood flowed. She slowed, and his claws racked across her belly. Then his jaws fixed on her throat, clamping shut, chewing, feeling the life slip away from her.

She was nourishment. He ate her, and the taste of her blood was good. Her spirit ran now with the other spirit animals, but her flesh would become his.

Weariness took him. It was time to sleep.

And then the true hunt would begin again.

21. With My Life

Aranloth and Kareste approached. The afternoon sun glittered on the gray sea behind them.

"Well?" Faran asked. "Have you reached a decision? Where do we go from here?"

"All choices may lead to ruin," Aranloth said. "There is no way to know the right path, for though I have the power of foresight and prophecy, it comes and goes as it will. For now, we walk in the dark."

"That's not very promising," Ferla said.

"It is what it is," the lòhren answered. "I can do no other. Yet still, my feeling is that we should head to a place known as Nurthil Wood. It's not far, and there, perhaps, we can find friends and help."

"They are good folk who live there," Kareste added. "Though wild and dangerous for outsiders to approach."

"But I've been there often," Aranloth said. "I've healed their sick and given good counsels. They are friendly to me, and will be to you also, I think."

It was all the same to Faran. He had no idea where to go or what to do. But he guessed that even Aranloth's feelings, while not the same as prophecy, might prove valuable in the end. At least, the legends always said that a lòhren's instincts were good. And there was also the old saying of *lòhren's luck* to describe a choice that ended up being particularly good, even if it did not seem so at the time of making.

"I'm happy to go to this Nurthil Wood," Faran said. "If not there, then where else? What place is safe for me?"

No one answered that, and he did not expect them to. They knew the answer as well as he did. Nowhere.

The afternoon sun cast long shadows over the headland as they found an old trail that wound away from the sea and back inland. Faran glanced one last time at the gray waters. Would he ever see their like again? And even the cries of the seagulls were like a lament for something lost as the trail descended to lower lands and the view from the headland disappeared.

They traveled through the night, but they rested frequently. They had been pushing themselves hard, and it was time to set a more leisurely pace. At least, while there was no sign of the enemy.

For a while, the paths they followed led them downhill, but this changed during the night. Now, they always moved uphill, and steep hills at that. Faran's legs grew weak, and his calves ached, but he kept going without complaint. The rests helped, but the hills would have been difficult even if he were fresh.

He liked this new country though, at least what he could see of it. They were climbing into a higher land, and one deeply wooded by ancient forests. It was rough country, full of treacherous crags, sudden drops and rocky outcrops thrusting from the earth like the towers of a city.

In such a place as this, it would be easier to lose pursuers, either those on foot or the enemy that was winged. And game would be plentiful, for there was little sign that people had ever passed this way. The trails Aranloth found were mostly beaten out by the passage of animals.

But there were signs of people. Here and there, they found the remnant of ancient paved roads, the stone cracked by centuries of frost and heat. Weeds grew up through them, and even trees. Yet still, these places were rare. For the most part, it was wild and rugged and dominated by the ancient forest.

It was not home. It could never replace Dromdruin, yet Faran began to think that a place such as this might be almost as good. So long as Lindercroft never found him.

That did not mean though that one day he would not seek the knight out. One way or another, Lindercroft would face justice for the crimes he had committed. No new home could ever allow Faran to forget the whispers of the dead in his dreams. He saw all the faces of the villagers in his sleep, both as they had been in life and as they had been in death.

At times, Aranloth walked well ahead, finding the way. He seemed cloaked in secrecy and aloofness. He always knew more than he said, and if he did not try to persuade Faran of anything, yet still Faran sensed he had a view, even if not spoken.

Kareste was similar, and she often trailed well behind, checking their backtrail and protecting them from that quarter. But from time to time she caught up to him and Ferla, and she did so soon after one of their rest breaks. Faran took the opportunity to talk to her.

"Tell me of Aranloth," he said quietly.

Kareste's gaze flickered to the back of the shadowy form ahead of them in the night.

"What would you know?"

"I know the legends. But what about him? What's he really like?"

She let down her hood and turned her gaze to him. "You already know the answer to that. He's as you have found him on this journey. Sometimes, he can be aloof, as he is now. But mostly, he's just like an ordinary man."

Faran thought on that. It was not what he really wanted to know, but he could not ask what he wanted to.

But Kareste seemed to know anyway. "But as I said, you know that already. What you want to know is something deeper, something more pressing. Yes?"

Faran nodded.

"You want to know if you're right to trust him as you have been doing so far?"

Faran nodded again. He did not want to speak. Asking that question seemed disloyal. Aranloth had risked his own life to help, and he did not have to do so. But did he have other motives?

Kareste turned her gaze back to the old man. "Trust is a strange thing. I may trust one person, and you another. Only we ourselves can give trust, and only we ourselves know why that trust is given. It's a personal choice. But in the case of Aranloth, I made mine long ago."

She pulled up her hood and covered her face again. "I trust him completely. He, and one other in all the world, I trust with my life. He has proven himself to me. And to others. He has many names in many lands. He's powerful. He has more courage than a warrior, and a store of compassion to match it. Yes, I trust him. But do you?"

She left them then, veering away to the left and flanking them for a while before falling back to her usual position in the rear. No enemy would creep up on them this night.

Faran considered her answer. It was a good one, but then the question became how much could he trust her? She was more of a stranger than Aranloth was.

He wondered, too, who this one other person was that she could trust with her life. It seemed so few, but then again, who did he trust with his? There was only one at the moment, and that was Ferla.

They rested before dawn, even sleeping for a while, but after the sun had risen and they had eaten a breakfast of their meager provisions, they began the march again.

As they went, the wood closed in on them even more. It was thicker, and older, and had a brooding feel to it. Oak dominated, but of a stunted kind in these rugged hills and ridges.

"Welcome to Nurthil Wood," a man said. And it was not Aranloth.

The lòhren, just a little ahead of the others was leaning on his staff, and he did not seem surprised.

"And a fine wood it is," answered the lòhren, "especially when the winter wind blows like daggers in the night, but venison is roasting at the front of a cave."

It was a slightly unusual reply, but when the first man laughed Faran understood why. It had been a password, a way of proving that Aranloth had been here before and was known.

The laughing man stepped out from behind a tree onto the track before them. In forest green he was dressed, with deer-hide boots and in his hand was a fine bow, strung with an arrow notched, though even as he came into sight he deftly slipped the arrow back into his quiver and unstrung the bow.

Faran knew a good archer by his movements, and one stood before him now.

"It's been a good while, Aranloth." He strode over and shook the lòhren's hand. It was clear that here they knew his real identity.

"So it has, Lord Greenwood. But won't you call over Berik from up in that tree? And Lorgril from behind yonder log? And who is it in those bushes over there? Jonlik, by the way those leaves tremble. He never could stand still for long."

Faran was surprised. He did not think it likely the man Aranloth was talking to had ever been a lord. Not here. But anything was possible. He was even more surprised at the other fellows who came out. He had not known they were there, so how could Aranloth have?

Lord Greenwood laughed, and he offered a bow with a grand flourish.

"Well spotted, Master Aranloth. Your senses are as sharp as ever. My men were well hidden."

"Indeed, but it takes no great skill to guess that the Lord of the Wood would be accompanied as he traveled his domain, nor the best hiding places for his men."

Lord Greenwood stroked his long mustache. He was a middle-aged man, and hardly old, but his mustache was white even if his hair was black.

"As you say, that took no great skill. But knowing their names? That's a different matter! But enough of that. A lòhren's secrets are his own. Or hers." He said the last with a careful glance at Kareste. "Now, you know my men. Will you introduce me to your companions?"

Faran knew instantly that whatever credibility Aranloth had here did not necessarily extend to his companions.

Aranloth offered a bow himself, and it was formal with more of a flourish than even Lord Greenwood had managed. He turned then to the rest of them.

"This is Faran. An archer of great skill, as even the bowmen of Nurthil Wood will admit if they see him loose his bow."

Faran felt the eyes of the lord on him, and there was interest there. But for all his friendly words and the easy laugh, there was a grim look to them.

"This is Ferla," Aranloth continued. "She has courage as I have seldom seen. She attacked an elù-drak to save her friend."

The lord's gaze shifted to her. There was no sign of a smile on his face now.

"A remarkable feat. Especially to do that and live. And we have heard rumor of dark creatures roaming the land once more. The old tales are told now every night while the cooking fires die down. And some claim to have seen things ... but enough of that."

"Best to remember the old tales," the lòhren said grimly. "Better still to travel abroad in groups and set a guard on any camp."

Lord Greenwood nodded at that. It was confirmation of the rumors he had heard, and advice at the same time. He looked like he took it to heart, though he offered no further comment.

"And this," Aranloth said, "is Kareste. A lòhren of talent and skill."

Lord Greenwood offered another bow. "Well met, to all of you. I'll take it as no coincidence that you show up when dark rumors flare to life. And no doubt there is a story to tell here. But I must hasten. My scouts have been sent out, and they'll return this night and tomorrow. I listen to rumors, but I prefer facts. I expect though that they'll bring ill news. But whatever their tidings, I must be there to hear them. But our main camp is presently well away from here."

He gazed at them all in turn, weighing them up. "It's my rule that no stranger enters Nurthil Wood. Not unless one who dwells here vouches for them. You, Aranloth, I have vouched for before. You are as one of us. Will you vouch for your friends?"

"I'll vouch for them," Aranloth agreed.

Lord Greenwood turned then to them. "And will you agree to obey the laws of Nurthil Wood while you shelter within it? And not to divulge, to anyone, what you see there and where our camps are?"

To this, they agreed one by one, and Faran knew it was no idle talk. Lord Greenwood was serious, and he looked deep into their eyes as they said the words. It was less like an agreement and more like an oath.

When they were done, Lord Greenwood spun on his toes. He gave a quick signal to his men, and they slipped into the forest. The rest of them followed.

As they moved ahead, Ferla drew close and whispered in Faran's ear.

"They're outlaws."

He had begun to think so too, though if they were they were of a kind that he had not heard of before. They were well led, organized and disciplined. Most of all Aranloth knew them, and they vouched for *him*. That was like a wolf saying a sheep was his best friend.

Yet the same applied in reverse. Aranloth was no sheep, but he was friendly with these people. There was certainly more to them than simple outlawry. Aranloth was a lòhren. He was a legend. He did not associate with thieves and worse.

Lord Greenwood, or as it appeared his men called him at most times, just Greenwood, was true to the words he spoke. He hastened.

They set a blistering pace through the forest, even if they just walked. But Greenwood was a tall man, and his stride long, so his walk could be fast.

He sent his three men out ahead, and they were rarely visible. Even less often were they heard. That was a remarkable show of woodsmanship, for they were traveling just as fast.

Faran was no stranger to woodsmanship. His livelihood had depended upon it, but he was impressed. He could learn from these people, and that was rare. In woodcraft at least, he had not met anyone in years who could teach him something new or a better way of doing things.

But then again, hunting called for great stealth, though it never called for speed at the same time. What these men were displaying was woodcraft, but more aligned to military skills than to hunting.

Late in the day, they reached a village. There were no roads to it, nor beaten tracks that someone might follow to find it. The inhabitants must take great care to come and go by different directions each time to avoid making any paths.

There were hidden platforms in the trees. It took Faran a while to spot them, but when he did he saw more and more. Lookouts were posted in those places, and they were armed with bows.

The village itself was a simple affair. There were rude huts of thatched roofs and bark-clad walls. In places, there were lean-tos and wattle fences for stock and gardens. Everything was neat and tidy, though. But one thing stuck out most. There were no chimneys nor sign of fire except in one place. This was beneath the spreading canopy of a massive oak whose branches and leaves would disperse smoke columns that otherwise would have been seen from afar.

Faran was surprised at the planning that had gone into this place. Lord Greenwood may or may not be a lord, but he certainly was a careful leader. And a good one.

Greenwood was hailed by many as he entered, and his three men dispersed to other duties. But for all that the villagers greeted him with friendliness, they kept sharp eyes on the rest. They were not a people who welcomed strangers easily.

An old man approached Greenwood. "About time," he wheezed through a straggly beard. "Some of the scouts have returned. They're at the meeting tree, waiting for you."

He limped away after that, not even sparing a glance for the rest of them.

Greenwood turned to them. "Duty calls," he said. "I'll fetch someone to look after you and find you a place to rest."

He left them then, following after the old man, but he spoke to a woman and pointed at them. She came over as Greenwood disappeared into the trees.

22. Ill Tidings

Faran waited with the others in a small hut. The woman that Greenwood had chosen to look after them provided several buckets of water for washing hands and faces. Soon after, she brought them food and beer.

The food was simple fare. Dried venison was the major part, salty but flavorful and well made. There were also bounties of the forest such as hazelnuts, chestnuts and several types of tuber. These were simply prepared, but wholesome. And the beer was as good as any Faran had ever had, though darker and sweeter than he was used to. He suspected there was honey in it, or the sap of a maple tree.

Night fell outside, and Aranloth lit a candle in its holder on the table.

"Do you think these people will help us?" Ferla asked.

Aranloth sat back, the flickering light of the candle casting strange shadows over his face.

"They'll help us as best they can, but they'll have their own problems soon enough, I expect. But we didn't come here for help. We came here to hide. And there are few better places."

As always, Faran sensed the old man knew more than he told, or at least guessed at more than he said. It was not a good feeling, and Greenwood's words about dark things walking the land came back to him.

The night pressed in from outside, and Faran had a bad feeling. But the four of them talked as they seldom had while traveling in the wild, and he was glad for that. It was a chance to get to know one another, and for all that he now mistrusted everybody, it was hard to mistrust lòhrens and Aranloth in particular. Of Ferla though, there was never and could never be any doubt. Her, he trusted with his life.

There was no door to the hut. Rather, a deer-hide flap served that purpose. Someone pulled it open now.

Lord Greenwood strode into the room. He did not look happy, but he was the sort of man who masked his feelings well. Faran would wager that if the sky had started raining fire, he would show only mild surprise.

"How went the meeting?" Aranloth asked.

Greenwood took the last remaining stump chair. "About as well as these things go. Ill tidings for the most part, and conflicting opinions. You know how meetings are."

"What were the ill tidings?"

"Just what we feared. Dark things are abroad. This village, and the others like it throughout Nurthil, are scared. Strange beasts have been seen, both in the woods and in the air. A shadow lies over the land, and not just Nurthil Wood. The scouts report rumors that much the same is happening in Faladir itself. There are whispers that the Kingshield Knights have fallen."

Greenwood said the last with a tone of question in his voice.

"The Kingshield Knights have fallen," Aranloth confirmed for him. "And the Morleth Stone works its power and gathers things of darkness to it."

"Will Faladir fall then to the shadow?"

"Maybe," agreed Aranloth. "But there is hope."

Greenwood stroked his long mustache. "You speak of the Seventh Knight?"

"I do."

"I've never believed much in prophecy. Time will tell though. In the meantime we'll do what we can and prepare as we may. It seems that not even Nurthil Wood will escape the attention of the king and the troubles of these times."

Aranloth's eyes sharpened at that last part. "What other ill tidings are there?"

"Dark beasts are not all that stir in the land. Men do also. And by men, I mean an army. It's camped on the edge of Nurthil Wood, less than fifteen miles away."

Greenwood shifted his gaze from Aranloth for the first time, and Faran felt his stare upon him. Somehow, Lindercroft had tracked him down again, or guessed where he would hide. Greenwood knew why that army was there, and what Lindercroft wanted.

Faran felt as though a noose were about his neck, getting tighter and tighter.

23. The Hypocrisy of Politics

Lindercroft waited at the center of the camp. A thousand men had joined him now, and it was a small army that he commanded.

He felt alive. With men to command, and victory within his grasp, the future of the Morleth Knights was secure.

The men were as nothing to him. They were not knights, nor did they necessarily support the new order of things in Faladir. But they knew how to obey orders, and that was all that was needed. For now.

Supposedly, they had been sent by the king. That at least was the rumor he had circulated. Their purpose was to respond to the threat of raiders. So the rumor went, the raiders had attacked a small village far away from Faladir. Dromdruin village it was called, and the army had been sent to track these men down and bring them to justice.

Lindercroft sipped at his watered wine, enjoying the shade cast by a flap raised from the front of his tent. He nearly laughed out loud. Such was the hypocrisy of politics. It would not do to admit that Dromdruin had been destroyed at the king's express order. No. Far better the population believed the king sought to bring raiders to justice. It was all a joke, but it was a serious one.

Anyone in power knew the use of politics. It was a tool to be used by the hands of the wealthy, ambitious or greedy. Whatever was said was usually the opposite of the truth. It was wolves giving speeches, forming committees and ruling in the name of wisdom and justice – all in order to have a secret supply of juicy lambs to eat. And no matter that the wolves learned to cook the lamb and eat it off a silver dish. They were still wolves.

Lindercroft stretched out his legs. Better to be a wolf than a lamb. But while politics had its uses, when the king secured true power over the land and all forces of possible opposition were destroyed, then the golden age would begin. Truth would replace politics, and a reign, firm but fair, would govern all lives equally.

He allowed himself a slight smile, but then cringed in pain. The welt over his face that the king had given him flared with agonizing sharpness, and he gritted his teeth against it. Against that, and the burning sensation in his eyes as though the fire lit in them had never gone out. For some reason, the king's punishment lingered longer than it ever had before.

Angrily, he muttered words of power, and the pain diminished again. Somewhat. What remained, he ignored, for men approached him. It would not do to let others see weakness in him. Those who ruled now, and those who would ascend to positions of undreamed-of power in the future, must separate themselves from ordinary people. Showing weakness undermined leadership.

The men were scouts, and when they reached him they gave their bows and waited on permission to speak. He signaled it with an impatient gesture of his finger.

"There is no news yet, my Lord. We have entered this place called Nurthil Wood, and found some stray inhabitants. They know nothing of the one you seek, but they say the wood is vast."

"Keep looking," Lindercroft told him. "The boy and his companions are there. Somewhere."

He looked away then, and that served as a dismissal. The scouts left, but he expected more through the days ahead. He was sure his quarry was in those woods. He felt it, and he had learned to trust the growing instincts of his magic.

And if the scouts did not find those he pursued, then the elù-drak would. Nothing and no one could hide from him for long.

He was troubled though. The scouts had gazed at his face as though seeing an actual welt there. That was impossible, for the spirit-pain the king inflicted was only illusionary. Unless his power had grown even greater.

That was disturbing, but he had little time to ponder it. A new pair of scouts arrived. Their report was the same as the previous one, and he grew impatient. Should whatever creature the king had summoned to hunt the boy find him first, it would lower his own standing before the king and the other knights. That would be intolerable.

He gave the scouts gold, and instructions. They were to buy whatever information they could from whatever inhabitants they found. And if gold failed to loosen tongues, then they were free to use whatever other methods worked. Sharp steel and burning coals were cheaper than gold, if slower.

The scouts left swiftly. Perhaps they were eager to undertake the task at hand, but Lindercroft felt their gaze on his face just as with the previous ones.

But in the end, none of it really mattered. He was Lindercroft, and a Morleth Knight. All things were possible, and if he felt the king's disfavor now, that would be remedied the moment the boy was dead.

He sat back and stretched out his legs again. Pain could be endured, and soon his mission would be accomplished. When that happened, there would be no thoughts of punishment. No. When that happened, he would receive a reward.

He looked around him at the camp. He had scouts in the wood, seeking information. They would find those they sought, sooner or later. And here, in the camp, were a thousand men keen to be the one to hack the boy's head off his shoulders. The same weight in gold was motivation that none of them would ignore.

Almost, he could pity the boy.

24. Advice is in Vain

Faran gave a slight nod. Greenwood knew, and there was no point in trying to hide the fact, even if the lord of these woods had not known.

"The army is after me."

Greenwood showed no surprise. He *had* known. But the look in his eyes was more one of respect for acknowledging the truth than distaste at what Faran's presence had brought on his people.

"Yes. They're after you. They're offering gold for information too. And I can tell you, gold is rare in Nurthil Wood."

"Am I safe here?"

Greenwood considered that. "You're probably safer here than most places. Certainly in this village and among my kin. But there are more people in this forest than you would think, and though they all fall under my rule, sooner or later someone will speak. Even if they haven't seen you themselves, word travels."

Faran knew that was true. He sensed the other man was being honest with him, but he could not discern his thoughts or wishes in the matter. Almost, he was being helpful. Maybe he had his own grudge against the king and the Kingshield Knights. Or maybe he had pieced together old tales and current events – and come to the conclusion that he was the seventh knight. Whether it was true or not mattered less than the fact that he had two lòhrens with him, and that made it *look* like it might be true.

"What will you do if Lindercroft's men come into the forest?"

Greenwood's gaze narrowed. "Ah, I should have guessed he would be behind it. I know *that* one."

Faran's guess had been right. There was a distinct tone of dislike there. Greenwood certainly held a grudge against the knights or even Lindercroft personally, but he kept it tightly to his chest and kept speaking.

"We have little enough here in the forest, and we have planned for such an event. Nurthil is large, and there are secret caves and valleys that even an army would take years to discover. And deer and other game is plentiful, not to mention we have stores of grain. We'll hide and not be found, at least for a long time."

Greenwood paused then, as though considering. "You can come with us. Perhaps word will not get out that you have entered the wood. And we can make you all look like one of us too. We can keep you in my family group. It's possible that Lindercroft may never find you."

Faran was humbled. Here was a stranger, already seemingly in some sort of exile, yet still willing to deepen that to help him. Or at least to help Aranloth help him.

But it was Aranloth who spoke. "You have proved a good friend, Lord Greenwood."

"As have you always," the other man replied.

Aranloth gripped his staff tightly. "Perhaps it's best to let young Faran think on it," he said. "He has some decisions to make, and none of them easy."

Greenwood stood. "A good idea. There's no great hurry. At least not tonight. But tomorrow, we all have decisions to make. My scouts are watching the army, and more reports will be coming in. We may have to leave here, and if we do, better tomorrow than the day after. That army is much closer than I like."

He left them then, and they were alone again.

"A good man, that Greenwood," Kareste said. "He thinks of his people first, but he's loyal to you as well," Kareste said, looking at Aranloth.

"I did him a favor once, a long time ago," the lòhren said.

Faran sensed there was more going on here than he knew, but he guessed something from the way Greenwood acted, and that he knew, and disliked, Lindercroft.

"He was a knight once himself, wasn't he? Greenwood, I mean."

Aranloth studied him carefully, and for the first time there was, perhaps, a hint of surprise in that penetrating gaze.

"You see more than most people, Faran. Yes, he was once a knight. He was of an age with Lindercroft, and they did not get on well. Lindercroft was in training, and Greenwood was already a knight. He was, shall we say, indiscreet with a lady in Faladir's court. In fact, she was related to the king. Anyway, the king discovered it and cast him from the order. That, I could accept. But the king sentenced Greenwood to death also. That, I could not. So I helped him escape."

"And Lindercroft took his place as a knight?"

"Exactly so. That, too, was against my wishes. But even then the king was prideful. I wonder now if he had already used the … but no matter. That's in the past."

"What I want to know though," Ferla said, "is what we're going to do now?"

Aranloth sighed. "A quick decision is a hasty decision. I suggest we all sleep on it overnight." Even as he said the words though, those all-seeing eyes met his gaze, and Faran knew the decision was ultimately going to be his.

It was not a good feeling. No matter what course of action he took now, it would end in trouble for himself and Ferla, or trouble for Greenwood and his people. If not, trouble for them all.

They talked deeper into the night, but of the choices before them, they spoke no more. When at last they went to bed, sleep was difficult to come by.

There were hard pallets in the hut, better perhaps than sleeping on the ground, but not by much. And a wind rose during the night, blowing through the tops of the trees and howling through the village. It sent leaves scattering, and branches rubbed against branches. The hut itself swayed and groaned, but it withstood the buffeting.

Faran lay awake, listening to the weather and thinking dark thoughts. Everything was always worse at night, and a deep malaise wound through his thoughts.

At last, he fell asleep. And it was a deep and dreamless sleep. He was more tired than he knew, and his body forced on him what it needed and ignored his racing mind.

When he woke, he found he was the last to do so. The sun was up, though only barely, and the raging wind had died down to a mere breeze, though it gusted from time to time as though trying to regain its power from last night.

The same woman who had brought them food yesterday did so again, and if she was not friendly she was not unfriendly either.

Given the trouble Faran had brought these people, that was better treatment than he deserved.

They ate their meal in silence, but when they were done, Aranloth spoke.

"Well, Faran, what do you wish to do? Take Greenwood up on his offer? Or shall we try our luck and slip away from Nurthil Wood, and hope to leave Lindercroft behind us once and for all?"

Faran knew what he would do. He did not much like it, but it was right.

"Neither of those things," he answered. "I'll not bring ruin on Greenwood and his people, even if they're willing to risk it in gratitude to you."

Kareste leaned forward, her eyes boring into him. "Then if not that, and not fleeing, then what?"

Faran met her gaze. "Fleeing, yes. But not straight away. At least not me. All of you, I think, should take the opportunity to disappear. And there will be one. I'll go by myself, and I'll find Lindercroft's men near the border of Nurthil Wood, and I'll let them see and pursue me. That way, I can lead them away from Greenwood and his people, and from you."

That was not what they were expecting, and there was dead silence for a moment.

"You're not going alone, Faran," Ferla said. Her voice was soft, but there was steel in it.

Faran did not answer her. He could not. So he turned instead to Aranloth.

"You know I'm right. I can't bring ruin on Nurthil Wood. Or on anyone else. What else could you advise me to do, but what I plan?"

Aranloth absently ran his hand along his staff. "I cannot advise," he said, "for advice is in vain. Who is to say, no matter how wise they are, what is the best way forward? But I can say this, and I will. Your choice *feels* right to me."

Ferla stood up. "He will *not* go alone."

Aranloth looked at her carefully, and he seemed pleased.

"I said his choice feels right, and it does. At least, in trying to save Nurthil Wood. And it's a good plan, for once the enemy sees him they'll certainly forget this forest. But I did not say he should do it alone. And it's doomed to failure without our help."

"I can't put anyone else in jeopardy because of me," Faran said.

Ferla looked at him sternly. "That's not your choice."

"And I agree with her," Aranloth said. "And it may be that not all my tricks are exhausted, and you'll certainly need a trick or two if your plan works. Otherwise you'll save Nurthil Wood by sacrificing your own life. A noble thing to do, but foolish when another plan might suffice."

Faran was not sure what other tricks the lòhren had. Nothing had worked so far, but it never paid to underestimate a lòhren. At least, that's what the legends said. They were at their most dangerous when their backs were to the wall.

At any rate, he had no chance to argue. Aranloth told them to get their things together, and he opened the flap at the entrance and walked through. They all followed him moments later.

Greenwood must have been waiting for them, because when they emerged Aranloth was already talking to him. But that did not last long. Soon Greenwood came over.

"I think you've made a good choice, Faran. A dangerous one, but good. Trust in Aranloth, and he'll see you through this."

Faran was not sure how. Lindercroft seemed like an unstoppable force, but this man had once been a knight, so he bowed. He did not have to agree with the man to show him the respect he had earned. Although Faran's feelings on that matter were mixed. He hated the knights, but his grandfather had been one.

But over and above being a knight, Greenwood had been willing to help. That earned him respect and gratitude.

All around them, there was a sense of threat hanging in the air. It was written on the faces of all they saw, and it was clear they all knew of Lindercroft's army.

Faran just wanted to go, and get things over and done with. But they waited a little while. Greenwood promised to replenish their food supplies, and he offered two scouts as well.

When they were ready, the scouts led them into the trees. They had seen Lindercroft's army, and knew this part of the wood well.

Greenwood waved them farewell, and then the village was soon gone and all sign of people vanished with it. There were just the trees, and the ghostly scouts ahead of them. But though he could not see it, the threat of the army out there infected Faran too. What he was about to do now was a challenge to it, and to the man who led it. That was the sort of challenge a man laid down at the risk of his life.

25. A Ring of Standing Stones

The scouts moved like ghosts ahead of them, and Faran and his companions followed, no less stealthily. But at one point, Kareste approached him, and she spoke softly.

"Yours is a bold plan," she told him. "Bold, like the thinking of a Kingshield Knight."

"I'm not a knight, nor ever will be," he replied. "But it's the right thing to do."

She gave no answer to that, and for his part he looked ahead only, following in the trail of Greenwood's scouts. He admired their skill, for they moved swiftly and silently. But he knew they would return back to the village when the enemy was close.

And the enemy was closer than they had thought. During the day, it had moved into the woods. They were still not far from the border though, and it seemed that the maneuver was more for show than anything else. It was intended, Aranloth surmised, to pressure those who lived in the forest to yield whatever information they had.

Faran wondered how good a tactic it was though. Certainly, it might serve its purpose. But on the other hand, Lindercroft would have feared to do so if he knew how well these people were led. Half his army could be destroyed by a surprise attack. Greenwood and his men had the skill, and the woods were all to their advantage.

The two scouts ahead of them came back. "We're here," one of them whispered. "The army is close, and a patrol is coming this way. Good luck."

With that, they melted into the trees once more and headed back toward Greenwood. No doubt, they would not go far though. Not yet. First, they would watch and learn whether or not this plan of Faran's worked, and if the enemy were lured out of the woods and away from Greenwood's people.

"Right," Faran whispered. "It's time to get this over and done with. Will you let me go on alone from here? There's no need for all of us to be seen."

"I don't think so," Aranloth answered. "And I may be able to help. Stand still everyone, and stay close together."

Whatever the lòhren intended, Faran could not guess. But he would have to do it swiftly. A little over a hundred yards away a flock of wood pigeons took to the sky, and it likely pinpointed where the patrol was.

Aranloth planted the tip of his staff against the ground. He muttered some strange-sounding words, and then he swept the staff around him in a slow-rising arc.

Nothing happened. But it did feel colder. Faran was about to speak, but the old man waved him to silence.

"Wait and see," he whispered.

Faran waited. His heart thumped in his chest, for the patrol must be close now, and they were all just standing there amid the trees.

But then he saw it. Tendrils of fog whispered up from the ground and wound about tree trunks and branches. Swift it climbed, thickening as it grew, creating a silvery gloom in the wood. It did not obscure their vision completely, but it halved it, and it was already difficult to see within the trees, though the forest was not thick here.

Somewhere ahead of them, muffled by the fog, came the sound of curses. It was the patrol, and they were very close now. This fog out of nowhere had surprised them, and they did not like it.

The sound of their passage was loud, and Faran knew exactly where they were. He moved ahead a little, and he drew an arrow onto his already strung bow.

The men came into sight. There were twelve. They had not seen him yet, but that was a matter of moments away. He knew that he should kill one of them now, or several, and he could, for he would not miss such targets. But killing men in cold blood was not his way, even if it meant there would be more to pursue.

He loosed the arrow. It sped through the air, and too late the enemy sensed something wrong. Just as they were looking at him, the arrow hit a man in the side of his helm. It would not kill him, and he would think for the rest of his life that he had been lucky, but it was Faran who had spared his life with skillful aiming.

"For Dromdruin!" Faran cried. If they had not known who he was before, they surely would now.

"Run," Aranloth commanded. And Faran and the others ran with him.

The fog deepened. Behind came the sound of horns blowing. Faran should have expected that. The patrol was not the only one, and there were other soldiers nearby. Answering horn calls came, and each sent a shiver up his spine.

There was a mad rush through the trees. Aranloth urged them to stay close, for if they got separated in the fog they would never find each other again.

But the fog helped too. The enemy pursued, but they would have a hard time seeing their quarry. And Aranloth led them in a loop, veering to the side and then heading back toward the edge of the wood.

Of Greenwood's scouts, there was no sign. But Faran guessed they were close by, hunkered down somewhere and watching. They would not interfere, and he did not blame them.

The chase wore on. Just as the first group seemed to lose them, a second stumbled upon them and loosed a shower of arrows. It was to no avail. With a sweep of her staff, Kareste sent a sheet of flame into the air and the shafts flared to bright lights and trailing ashes the moment they hit that fiery wall.

Faran stumbled, but Ferla was at his side helping him regain his balance before he knew it. Then they sped on, a mad music of horns behind them announcing their location to all who could hear.

The forest grew even sparser, and then they were out and into the open. Green grass lay beneath their boots. An open sky was above, but the world was blanketed in fog thicker than it had been in the forest.

To the west, the ground dipped lower, and the fog lay in that declivity like a slow-drifting river. But rising above it, a mile or more away, hunkered the broad shoulders of a hill.

"There!" Aranloth said, pointing at the hill with his staff. "That way lies our safety. Mark it well!"

But he did not wait. He strode ahead into the gloom, and they followed him.

It was cold and clammy in the fog. More than that, Faran could feel the magic in the air about him. Dromdruin had often been blanketed in fogs, but none had ever felt like this.

"Stay close," Aranloth commanded again, his voice no more than a whisper through the thick air.

All sound was muffled, and they tried to make as little as possible. Behind them, at first, they heard the noise of pursuit. But it trailed after, and then veered to the side. Soon, there was no sound at all, muffled or otherwise.

Of the hilltop that was their destination, nothing was visible. How Aranloth could possibly find it, he did not know. But the lòhren was full of surprises, and he had expressed no doubt that they would reach it, so Faran was willing to trust in that.

It seemed his trust was well placed. After what felt like a long time moving through the fog, Faran noticed that the ground was beginning to slope upward. He was not sure at first, but then swiftly the angle increased.

They were climbing the hill. The fog about them thinned a little, but did not dissipate. Currents of air moved and eddied, and the fog shifted one way and then another. Sometimes it looked like it was about to give way, and then it drew in again.

"We're near the top," Aranloth informed them. "Be wary. Lindercroft is many things, but none of them is stupid. He may have sent men to the crest as lookouts, or he may even be there himself."

Faran's bow was still strung, and he felt the arrows in his quiver for reassurance, but did not nock one. Prudence was one thing, giving way to panic another. He would wait until he saw an enemy before he took any action.

But there was no sign of one. Through wispy strands of fog, they climbed to the clear air at the top of the hill. It was bare of trees, and the grass was short and green. There was nothing there but a ring of ancient standing stones.

"The Ring of Carcur-halioth," Aranloth intoned, and his voice was somber.

Faran had heard of such rings before. They belonged to the ancient past, and before all the Camar tribes had migrated eastward, they had worshipped and held ceremonies about such structures. But they had abandoned the practice when they came into contact with the immortal Halathrin, and he had not heard of any built around Faladir.

Almost, it seemed, Aranloth read his mind. "This ring was built in an age before the last age. The Letharn constructed it, and though it looks like any other ring of standing stones, it could not be more different."

Faran seemed to remember hearing some legend of an ancient people whose empire had fallen long before even the Shadowed Wars. Perhaps they had delved the passages in the headland by the sea.

"But why bring us here?" he asked. "Standing stones cannot hide us from the enemy."

Kareste, her brown-green eyes flashing with amusement, laughed softly but did not speak.

"Your ancestors built rings of standing stones," Aranloth explained. "And they built them in places where the old powers of the earth ran strong. The Letharn did the same before them, but *they* knew how to harness those old forces."

"Harness them for what?"

"For Traveling," Kareste answered. "Now let Aranloth do what he must. The Ring must be activated, and the enemy have not forgotten us."

Faran fell silent, but he watched closely. He understood now why Aranloth had hope of escape, but he could have mentioned this Traveling business earlier.

Or had that been a test? Not for the first time he had the odd feeling that Aranloth was studying him in some way to see what he was made of. But that might be too presumptuous as well. Holding back secrets came as second nature to lòhrens in the same way that arrows hissed as they flew through the air. It was just in their nature.

Aranloth moved among the stones, muttering words of power. To each, he also rested a hand and a faint white light pulsed from his palm. When he removed it, the glow of magic remained on the stone, spreading over it.

Faran noticed something else too. The old man did not go to the stones from one to the other in accordance with which was closer. No, he moved, seemingly randomly, sometimes crossing the circle fully and then going back again. It was not random at all, and followed some ritual or order. Nor did he place his hand on the same spot on each stone. Sometimes, he reached up high to touch them, and other times he bent low.

Whatever he was doing, Faran saw the effects. Light began to swirl among the stones, jumping from one to another. It grew stronger and faster, and soon it seemed that the very stones were striding in a circle around them. And he felt some force in the earth. It was like a low grinding noise, below the edge of his hearing. Almost, he thought he felt it thrumming up through his boots.

"You feel it, don't you?" Kareste whispered in his ear.

"I feel something, but I don't know what. Magic, I suppose. But why shouldn't I feel it?"

Her face was a mask of inscrutability, but she gazed at him out of those beautiful eyes with the hint of a knowing look. Yet still, she offered no answer.

The mist crept up the hill toward them, swirling and flowing, and then suddenly it stilled.

"To the center of the circle!" Aranloth cried.

Even as they moved, a sudden wind blew. It tore the fog about the hill to shreds, and sent it whirling into oblivion. Lindercroft had come. He was revealed now, and he was a figure of terror. His helm gleamed on his head. His great sword was drawn, and a cold fire flickered along its edge. Magic. Magic to counter Aranloth's, and Faran felt a shadow creep over his heart.

About the knight were scores of warriors. But they seemed as nothing compared to Lindercroft himself, revealed now as both a warrior and a sorcerer of might.

But he was a murderer too, and Faran had sworn to avenge Dromdruin. He notched an arrow, drew and fired in one motion. This time, he sent the arrow winging with the intention of killing. He aimed for the weak spot between helm and chainmail coif, and even as the shaft leaped away, he knew his aim was good.

But Lindercroft was no ordinary man. He swayed to the side and his sword flashed in an arc of fire. It shattered the arrow into pieces.

And then the knight lifted high his blade, and lightning jagged from its tip. It tore into the ring of standing stones.

Aranloth was bent low, hastily muttering more words of power with his hand upon the last stone. But whatever magic he was invoking with the ring was not yet complete.

Kareste was there though, leaping before the others and spinning her staff. A shield was thrown up, a thing of shimmering blue flame. Against it the lightning struck, and thunder boomed. The earth trembled, and one of the standing stones split in the middle, but did not fall.

Then, with a suddenness that caught Faran by surprise, the ring of stones spun faster and whirred. Lindercroft faded from his vision, and the world outside the stones became transparent and ephemeral.

The look on Lindercroft's face was one of despairing anguish, and Faran knew that at last they had escaped him.

Dizziness swamped him, and he fell to the ground. But even as he did so he saw a dark form come from behind the enemy soldiers. It leapt and bounded, and then vaulted itself with astonishing speed into the center of the ring.

It was a thing of shadow and flesh. Claws it had, to rend flesh. Fangs it had, to kill. It was part beast, part man and part a thing of magic.

And all its attention was on him.

The creature tumbled and rolled as it landed within the circle, but it came swiftly to its feet, first on four and then on two legs. It was death, and Faran knew, beyond doubt, that it had come to claim him.

It sprang toward him even as he fumbled for an arrow. But the magic of the standing stones reached its peak now.

Darkness enclosed the circle, blacker than the tomb. And it felt as though the earth moved, spinning with the ring of stones and Traveling.

Faran fell to the ground. Or it swept up toward him and knocked him down. Either way, the blackness took him, and he drifted on a wave of magic, half awake and half asleep. But completely vulnerable until the magic of the standing stones ran its course.

Thus ends *The Seventh Knight*. The Kingshield series continues in book two, *The Sorcerer Knight*, where Faran must confront ultimate evil.

THE SORCERER KNIGHT
BOOK TWO OF THE KINGSHIELD SERIES
COMING SOON

Amazon lists millions of titles, and I'm glad you discovered this one. But if you'd like to know when I release a new book, instead of leaving it to chance, sign up for my new release list. I'll send you an email on publication.

Yes please! – Go to www.homeofhighfantasy.com and sign up.

No thanks – I'll take my chances.

Dedication

There's a growing movement in fantasy literature. Its name is noblebright, and it's the opposite of grimdark.

Noblebright celebrates the virtues of heroism. It's an old-fashioned thing, as old as the first story ever told around a smoky campfire beneath ancient stars. It's storytelling that highlights courage and loyalty and hope for the spirit of humanity. It recognizes the dark, the dark in us all, and the dark in the villains of its stories. It recognizes death, and treachery and betrayal. But it dwells on none of these things.

I dedicate this book, such as it is, to that which is noblebright. And I thank the authors before me who held the torch high so that I could see the path: J.R.R. Tolkien, C.S. Lewis, Terry Brooks, David Eddings, Susan Cooper, Roger Taylor and many others. I salute you.

And, for a time, I too shall hold the torch high.

Appendix: Encyclopedic Glossary

Note: the glossary of each book in this series is individualized for that book alone. Additionally, there is often historical material provided in its entries for people, artifacts and events that are not included in the main text.

Many races dwell in Alithoras. All have their own language, and though sometimes related to one another the changes sparked by migration, isolation and various influences often render these tongues unintelligible to each other.

The ascendancy of Halathrin culture, combined with their widespread efforts to secure and maintain allies against elug incursions, has made their language the primary means of communication between diverse peoples.

This glossary contains a range of names and terms. Many are of Halathrin origin, and their meaning is provided. The remainder derive from native tongues and are obscure, so meanings are only given intermittently.

Often, names of Camar and Halathrin elements are combined. This is especially so for the aristocracy. Few other tribes of men had such long-term friendship with the immortal Halathrin as the Camar, and though in this relationship they lost some of their natural culture, they gained nobility and knowledge in return.

List of abbreviations:

Cam. Camar

Comb. Combined

Cor. Corrupted form

Hal. Halathrin

Leth. Letharn

Prn. Pronounced

Alithoras: *Hal.* "Silver land." The Halathrin name for the continent they settled after leaving their own homeland. Refers to the extensive river and lake systems they found and their wonder at the beauty of the land.

Aranloth: *Hal.* "Noble might." A lòhren of ancient heritage. Travels Alithoras under different names and guises.

Arach Nedular: *Leth.* "Bright light (usually but not always from a celestial object) over tossing waters – translates as moon over the sea, but some render it wonderous city over the sea." A port city of the Letharn. Famed in the ancient world for its beauty. Slowly destroyed by rising waters and now, mostly, sunk beneath the waves.

Berik: *Cam.* "Ber – a fish knife and ik – an artisan." An outlaw dwelling in Nuatha Wood under the rule of Lord Greenwood.

Camar: *Cam. Prn.* Kay-mar. A race of interrelated tribes that migrated in two main stages. The first brought them to the vicinity of Halathar, homeland of the immortal Halathrin; in the second, they separated and established cities along a broad stretch of eastern Alithoras. Faladir is one such city.

Camarelon: *Cam.* A city established by migrating Camar tribes. They retained more of their traditional cultural values and were less influenced by the Halathrin. The city they built is not as grand as other Camar cities, but it still became wealthy via profitable trade.

Carcur-halioth: *Leth.* An ancient ring of standing stones constructed by the Letharn. Named after one of their great magicians, Carcur. His abode was in Arach Nedular, but he had great need to travel widely through the Letharn empire, which was vast. He did not invent Traveling, but he discovered how to construct a ring of standing stones that made the process far less dangerous.

Cardoroth: *Cor. Hal. Comb. Cam.* A Camar city, often called Red Cardoroth. Some say this alludes to the red granite commonly used in the construction of its buildings, others that it refers to a prophecy of destruction.

Careth Tar: *Cor. Hal.* "Careth Tar(an) – Great Father." Title of respect for the leader of the lòhrens. This has always been, and remains, Aranloth.

Conduil: *Cam.* Etymology obscure. The first king of Faladir. He broke the Siege of Faladir and founded the order of Kingshield Knights, of which he was the first.

Dardenath: *Cam.* "Spear of the water – a boat built for speed rather than fishing or cargo. Usually a warship." A farmer of Dromdruin Valley. Many names of Faladir origin relate to the sea, for they were a seagoing folk before they spread far from the ocean to settle farming lands.

Darr-harran: *Leth.* An ancient land at the far south of the Letharn empire that once produced esteemed wines on its arid slopes.

Drom Hairn: *Cam.* "Valley whisperer." A stream of Dromdruin Valley.

Dromdruin: *Cam.* "Valley of the ancient woods." One of many valleys in the realm of Faladir. Home of Faran, and birthplace throughout the history of the realm of many Kingshield Knights.

Durnlik: *Cam.* "Settlement amid the trees." A neighboring village of Dromdruin.

Elves: See Halathrin.

Elù-drak: *Hal.* "Shadow wings." A creature of the dark. Deadly dangerous, and used by sorcerers to gather information and assassinate chosen victims. The female of the species is the most dangerous, having the power to inspire terror and bend victims to her will. Few can resist. Of old, even great warriors succumbed and willingly let the creature take their life. One of the more terrible creatures of the old world.

Elùdurlik: *Hal.* "Shadow hunter." A type of summoning. Formed of a melding of dark magic and the thoughts of the summoner. Instilled with a driving purpose that it can never ignore, and dies once that purpose is achieved.

Elùgai: *Hal. Prn.* Eloo-guy. "Shadowed force." The sorcery of an elùgroth.

Elù-haraken: *Hal.* "The shadowed wars." Long ago battles in a time that is become myth to the scattered Camar tribes.

Elùdrath: *Hal.* "Shadowed lord." Once, a lòhren. But he succumbed to evil and pursued forbidden knowledge and powers. He created an empire of darkness and struck to conquer all Alithoras during the elù-haraken. He was defeated, but his magic had become greater than any ever known. Some say he will return from death to finish the war he started. Whether that is so, no one knows. But the order of lòhrens guard against it, and many evils that served him still yet live.

Elùgroth: *Hal.* "Shadowed horror." A sorcerer. They often take names in the Halathrin tongue in mockery of the lòhren practice to do so.

Esgallien: *Hal.* "Es – rushing water, gal(en) – green, lien – to cross: place of the crossing onto the green plains." A river ford in southern Alithoras after which one of the great Camar cities was named.

Faladir: *Cam.* "Fortress of Light." A Camar city founded out of the ruinous days of the elù-haraken.

Faran: *Cam.* "Spear of the night – a star. A name of good luck. Related to the name Dardenath, though of a later layer of linguistic change." A young hunter from

Dromdruin valley. His grandfather was a Kingshield Knight, though not the first of their ancestors to be so.

Ferla: *Cam.* "Unforeseen bounty." A young hunter from Dromdruin valley.

First Knight: The designated leader of the Kingshield Knights.

Halath: *Hal.* King of the Halathrin. He died long ago. He led his people on their exodus to Alithoras, and was revered and loved as a great ruler. Originally, one of the main opponents of Elùdrath.

Halathar: *Hal.* "Dwelling place of the people of Halath." The forest realm of the immortal Halathrin.

Halathrin: *Hal.* "People of Halath." A race of elves named after an honored lord who led an exodus of his people to the land of Alithoras in pursuit of justice, having sworn to defeat a great evil. They are human, though of fairer form, greater skill and higher culture. They possess a unity of body, mind and spirit that enables insight and endurance beyond the native races of Alithoras. Said to be immortal, but killed in great numbers during their conflicts in ancient times with the evil they sought to destroy. Those conflicts are collectively known as the Shadowed Wars.

Halls of Lore: Essentially, a library within the stronghold of the lòhrens in northern Alithoras. It serves as a repository for the known history of humanity and the wisdom of the ages. Founded by Careth Tar, also known as Aranloth.

Har-harat: *Leth.* An energy point of the body just below the navel. Used as a focus for meditation and to replenish the body's vital force. By meditation on this point, the physical body and the spiritual essence are unified. Used by both warriors and mystics.

Herna: *Cam.* "Horned fish." The smith of Dromdruin Village.

Hrolgar: *Cam.* "Sharks of the air." Mythical carrion birds, though Camar legend claims they flew above the great army that besieged Faladir after the elù-haraken, and fought against the defenders.

Immortals: See Halathrin.

Jonlik: *Cam. Comb. Hal.* "Happy hunter – dolphin." An outlaw dwelling in Nuatha Wood under the rule of Lord Greenwood.

Kareste: *Hal.* "Ice unlocking – the spring thaw." A lòhren of mysterious origin. Friend to Aranloth, but usually more active farther north in Alithoras than Faladir.

Kingshield Knights: An order of knights founded by King Conduil. Their sacred task is to guard the indestructible Morleth Stone from theft and use by the evil forces of the world. They are more than great warriors, being trained in philosophy and the arts also. In addition to their prime function as guards, they travel the land at whiles dispensing justice and offering of their wisdom and council.

Letharn: *Hal.* "Stone raisers. Builders." A race of people that in antiquity conquered most of Alithoras. Now, only faint traces of their civilization endure.

Lindercroft: *Cam.* "Rising mountain crashes – a wave rolling into the seashore." A Kingshield Knight. Youngest of the order.

Lòhren: *Hal. Prn.* Ler-ren. "Knowledge giver – a counselor." Other terms used by various nations include wizard, druid and sage.

Lòhren-fire: A defensive manifestation of lòhrengai. The color of the flame varies according to the skill and temperament of the lòhren.

Lòhrengai: *Hal. Prn.* Ler-ren-guy. "Lòhren force." Enchantment, spell or use of mystic power. A manipulation and transformation of the natural energy inherent in all things. Each use takes something from the user. Likewise, some part of the transformed energy infuses them. Lòhrens use it sparingly, elùgroths indiscriminately.

Lord Greenwood: The ruler of Nurthil Wood. Once a Kingshield Knight, but unjustly outlawed by the king. Great enmity exists between himself and Lindercroft, who took his place in the order. Upon a time, he was tutored by Faran's grandfather. His true name is Caludreth.

Lorgril: *Cam.* "Boat wright." An outlaw dwelling in Nurthil Wood under the rule of Lord Greenwood.

Magic: Mystic power. See lòhrengai and elùgai.

Morleth Stone: *Hal.* "Round stone." The name signifies that such a stone is not natural. It is formed by elùgai for sorcerous purposes. The stone is strengthened by arcane power to act as a receptacle of enormous force. Little is known of their making and uses except that they are rare and that elùgroths perish during their construction. The stone guarded by the Kingshield Knights in Faladir is said to be the most powerful of all that were created. And to be sentient.

Nuatha: *Cam.* "Silver wanderer – a stream." A vagabond healer that travels widely throughout Faladir.

Nurthil Wood: *Cam.* "Dark secrets." A great forest north of Faladir. Home to outlaws and disaffected from the wide lands all around. Once, a stronghold of the forces of darkness, but cleansed by succeeding kings of Faladir.

Olek-nas: *Leth.* "The third eye." An energy point on the body between the eyebrows. Maintained to be a center of rationality and calm. Once a practitioner of the meditative arts "opens" this energy center, they are said to be able to look upon the world and see it for what it is with emotional detachment. Used in both the mystic and the warrior arts.

Osahka: *Leth.* "The guide – specifically a spiritual or moral guide." A title of enormous reverence and respect. Applied to Aranloth for his role as spiritual leader of the Kingshield Knights.

Shadow Hunter: See Elùdurlik.

Shadowed Lord: See Elùdrath.

Shadowed Wars: See Elù-haraken.

Six Knights, the: A range of hills standing above Dromdruin Valley. Named after the legendary knights. Many landmarks throughout Faladir are named after the knights, for they were well known and traveled widely.

Sorcerer: See Elùgroth.

Sorcery: See elùgai.

Sword of the Halathrin: A title of honor bestowed upon humanity by the Halathrin. But also descriptive. Humanity eventually formed the greater part of the armies of the elves during the elù-haraken.

Traveling: A feat of lòhrengai of the highest order. It enables movement of the physical body from one location to another via entry to the void in one place and exit in a different. Only the greatest wizards are capable of it, but it is never used. The risk of death is too high. But use of specially constructed rings of standing stones makes it safer.

Ùhrengai: *Hal.* "Original force." The primordial force that existed before substance or time.

Way of the Sword: The martial aspect of the training of a Kingshield Knight.

Wizard: See lòhren.

About the author

I'm a man born in the wrong era. My heart yearns for faraway places and even further afield times. Tolkien had me at the beginning of *The Hobbit* when he said, ". . . one morning long ago in the quiet of the world . . ."

Sometimes I imagine myself in a Viking mead-hall. The long winter night presses in, but the shimmering embers of a log in the hearth hold back both cold and dark. The chieftain calls for a story, and I take a sip from my drinking horn and stand up . . .

Or maybe the desert stars shine bright and clear, obscured occasionally by wisps of smoke from burning camel dung. A dry gust of wind marches sand grains across our lonely campsite, and the wayfarers about me stir restlessly. I sip cool water and begin to speak.

I'm a storyteller. A man to paint a picture by the slow music of words. I like to bring faraway places and times to life, to make hearts yearn for something they can never have, unless for a passing moment.

Printed in Great Britain
by Amazon